(ROMAN A' CLEF)

MY FATHER'S DAUGHTER

A short fictional novel

SANDRA V. ALLISON

authorHOUSE®

AuthorHouse™
1663 Liberty Drive
Bloomington, IN 47403
www.authorhouse.com
Phone: 833-262-8899

Published by AuthorHouse 09/02/2020

ISBN: 978-1-7283-6854-2 (sc)
ISBN: 978-1-7283-6432-2 (e)

Library of Congress Control Number: 2020913819

Print information available on the last page.

Introduction

*S*ometimes, in the arena of human life there may be an area that leaves
you feeling incomplete or deficient. You may have experienced this by
way of a challenging educational goal, a disappointing relationship, a
broken promise or a bad decision. You may have always wanted to come to
terms with it, but you didn't. Sometimes, you settle and just put a comma down
and move on. As Sandy lived from day to day there was an inner gnawing that
kept drawing her back to that area of discontent in her life. She would discover
that it would take years before she could remove the comma and put a period.
Daily, she had to live with the incompleteness and try to move on. She did,
but that wasn't always easy and it wasn't always because of her.

Acknowledgements

To my Lord Jesus Christ who makes all things possible in my life!

I am Grateful! To the many persons that have supported, encouraged and prayed for me while I worked on this book. Some of you pulled the late night shift of brainstorming or provided technical support. While others of you gave me ideas unknowingly and pushed me forward when I was at an impasse. I could dedicate this book to many and you know who you are!

To my only son, Gregory, whom I love dearly

And

My late husband,
(Reverend) Wilton E. Belford Jr.

Chapter One

I sat in the doctor's office waiting for my name to be called. I don't know why I didn't change doctors. Dr. Nuwi was always backed up. I got mad at myself for allowing him to take up so much of my time. I hated to waste time, but I waited because he was such a good doctor, the best. As I sat there and looked around the waiting room at the other patients, I could see by the expressions on their faces that each one had a story. Some looked like the weight of the world was upon their shoulders while others looked like they weren't even in this world. Yet behind their eyes were untold, sorted stories of their life's journey. Each one, given the opportunity, would probably tell their story to whoever would listen. I had a story too. I didn't know all the details of my story but I was looking forward to finding the missing pieces.

The nurse, Bertha, swung the door open and shouted "Mrs. Walls, come with me please". A short grayed hair lady grabbed her purse and quickly stepped behind her. Bertha was an unpredictable person you never knew what her mood would be when you arrived at Dr. Nuwi's office. I guess it depended on how the day was going for her. It didn't matter to me because I set the tone for my visit. I didn't let her tell me what kind of visit it was going to be, based on her mood. As I continued to sit there and looked around the room my eyes got heavy and my mind left the office and journeyed way back to a time when I first started going to a doctor regularly, I was pregnant. **"Ms. Allis"**, the sound of Bertha's voice quickly snapped me back to the here and now "You can come on back". I gathered my things and followed her through the door. "How are you today?" she said. "Oh, I am doing pretty good for an old woman". She laughed. I knew then that it was going to be a good visit. She took my blood pressure, weighed me, and took my temperature. She asked me if I was in any pain and all of the preliminary stuff. We talked a little bit about her kids and my job and then she told me that the doctor would be right with me. I knew what that meant, another twenty minutes. I would usually take out a book that I was reading or do some paper work from my job, but today I just wanted to lay back on the examination table and rest. As I laid there on the table, my body began to relax. Again my thoughts began to drift. I thought about the poem that I read called "Those Little Things", you know, those little things that were big nuisances. All the makings of what could be a hectic week were rolled up into today. I was exhausted. I could feel myself beginning to nod off when I heard Dr. Nuwi opening the examination room door. "Ms. Allis, how are you doing today?" he said with a big smile across his face. I glanced at my watch before I replied. That would help me determine how good I was doing. "Not too bad" I said. Dr. Nuwi was from Africa. He was short in stature and always seemed to have something on his mind. He was educated here in the states and was a modern day workaholic. He would ask me questions that he already knew the answer to. Dr. Nuwi would always have me do blood work before my visit, so he had already read my results and knew what I was doing right and what I needed to tighten up on. As he turned to read my chart he said" How are you doing with your diet?" I looked at him with wide eyes and said" Dr. Nuwi, do it look like I have been on a diet?' He laughed out loud and we began the usual dialogue about what I needed to do and what would be helpful. He did my examination and we talked about some concerns that I had and what my blood work reflected. He finished with some instructions and a new prescription for the problem that I had developed. I thought to myself, just what I needed another condition and some more medication for it! He tried to encourage me about my diet, gave me another one of his big smiles, and reminded me to make my follow-up appointment before I left. I got dressed, opened the door, and saw Bertha coming down the hall. "You all finished?" she said as she looked up. "Yes, he wants me to make a follow-up appointment". "Okay you can see Dawn and I will call your prescription in if you want me to, just give me a minute, I'll be right with you" she said in a hurried voice. I waited at the receptionist's desk for her. The receptionist, Dawn, gave me a three-month follow-up appointment and Bertha called in my prescription. I thanked them both and left the office. As I walked to my car I checked my watch because I was meeting the girls for dinner. I didn't want to be late, although I knew that Marva would be, and Dessa would be on edge. They were my two best friends. We enjoyed our times together. We were each different, yet alike in many ways. We all loved the Lord and tried to live our lives as God would have us do. Although for me, some days were harder than others. Today was one of those days.

I started my car up and begin making my way to the restaurant. Traffic wasn't too bad and I arrived at the restaurant a little early. As I sat in my car on the restaurants' parking lot with my head back, I tried to release some of my stress. As I replayed the events of the day, in my mind, I recalled the heated exchange that I had with my co-worker, Ms. Eastman, this morning. I knew when it happened that my spirit would be disturbed for the whole day. She knew how to push the wrong buttons in me. I got angry with myself because I allowed her to take me out of my zone. She was a wolf in sheep clothing and always wanted to play the victim. I was sick of her. She was probably one of the reasons why I couldn't get my blood pressure down.

As I continued to sit in my car, I remembered the encounter. When I got to work, Ms. Eastman was standing at my office door looking agitated. She never said good morning or how are you doing, she just blurted out, "I need to talk to you" in her bossy way. I said "and good morning to you" as I proceeded to unlock my office door. I entered my office, put down my briefcase, and put away my purse. She was right on my heels demanding my immediate attention. "Why did you give Mrs. Hillary the supplies that I ordered for my area?" she shouted out loud enough for the whole area to hear. "What are you talking about Ms. Eastman? " I replied. Ms. Eastman was the kind of co-worker that always kept something going. She thrived on drama. She had been a thorn in my side for years. I knew that she was jealous of me; I just didn't know why. Maybe it was because I got the position that she thought she should have gotten. I was the Unit Department Supervisor. I was responsible for what went on in the department from ordering equipment to approving time off. "Mrs.

Eastman, I think that you have your facts incorrect. The supplies ……". "I know that you did that because I know what I ordered for my area". She cut me off before I could complete my sentence. "Mrs. Eastman," I said after taking a very deep breath, "give me some time and let me check your invoice against the supplies and the invoice that I have to see if there has been a mistake". I wanted to tell her to get the hell out of my office, but I knew then that I would have to hit her also. Plus I wasn't trying to act ugly with her this morning. She insisted that the supplies were hers as she went to take a seat in the chair that was in front of my desk. I thought to myself, now this hussy is really trying my patience. Didn't I say that I would need some time? She goes and sits her butt down in a chair. I said again in a very controlled voice" give me some time and I will check". "Well, I need to know now before Mrs. Hillary starts going through my stuff". "Well, I really don't have time to address this issue right now because I am on my way to a meeting in about ten minutes, but I promise to get back to you". "That's the problem; you are too busy to handle the more important things in this department. Every time I need something I gotta wait" she said with her smart, sarcastic mouth. She had said enough, in fact she had said too much! "Get out of my office" I said very directly "I will get to it when I can. You aren't the only person in this department that has needs, and you are right, they pay me to be busy and I choose what is important and what gets my immediate attention". As I grabbed my keys off of my desk and directed her out of my office door I ended with "and this is not one of those matters. I will get back to you later.

As I started down the hall I realized that I had allowed her to take me out of my zone. I had to pray and regroup before I went into my meeting. Our early morning encounter turned into an unprofessional exchange, and I admit, I was upset with myself because I permitted her to awake the old woman in me. Not only did the old woman wake up, but she also stood straight up, changed her tone of voice and her facial expression too! {Breathe}…Okay, I messed that encounter up. "Good morning Ms. Allis," I heard a pleasant cheery voice say, that snapped me back to myself, "Good Morning Ms. Fisher" I said. Ms. Fisher was a new employee. She was a pleasant young lady and I liked her. I took another deep breath before I entered into the room where the meeting was being held and whispered a prayer to ask the Lord to forgive me for my outburst towards Ms. Eastman, even though I felt like she deserved it. I knew that I would have to adjust my attitude before I dealt with her later.

Dessa tapped on my car window arousing me from my thoughts. I had my eyes closed and my doors locked. She spoke, "Hey Sandy "and then she asked the inevitable question, "Where is Marva?" I rolled my window down to tell her what she already knew, "Girl you know that Marva is going to be, late". "You may as well get on in and take a load off of your feet". "No baby, let's go on in and get our table before it get too crowded". I grabbed my purse and locked my car. When we entered the restaurant we checked out the atmosphere. There was a lot of chatter and music playing in the background. The hostess welcomed us and Dessa told her that we wanted to be seated in a booth and was expecting another guest. She led us to our table and said that our waitress would be with us shortly. Marva was late for most things except a plane, train or a scheduled bus. We knew that about her, and we loved her anyway.

Dessa and I settled in and started our small talk about the day. Dessa was the girlfriend that challenged me to find my self-esteem and self-worth. Most people would not believe that I struggled with that as a youth and as a young adult. I always had a sense of not being good enough. Whew, I am glad that I overcame that! When I met Dessa she helped me see myself in a more positive light. I kind of struggled with the things that other people saw as negative things in my life, my weight, complexion, height, tone of voice, kinky hair; you know the things that other people have problems with and try to make them your problems. In our friendship she looked pass those things and encouraged me to focus on the opposites of those negatives. This was who I was, and the reality of it was that I didn't want to be surrounded by individuals that couldn't accept me for who I really was. I spent a lot of time growing up trying to fit in. It was good to be accepted with my deep dark chocolate complexion, my plump curvy body frame, my healthy kinky hair and my voice that commanded attention when I spoke. I learned to love me through her encouragement and support. She was my oyster friend, tough exterior but a precious interior. Dessa was smart and secure within herself. She had a sense of directness that sensitive people probably wouldn't appreciate. She had a wonderful sense of humor. We could see certain things and find the humor in them and laugh about it over and over. We both had our faults, but we genuinely liked and loved each other. In Christ I was free and in our friendship I was liberated.

Marva still hadn't arrived when the waitress came back to the table to check on us, so we asked for a few more minutes. I could tell that Dessa was a little bothered that Marva hadn't arrived. "Where is Marva? Didn't she pick the time?" Dessa and I both were sticklers about time. She was regal, a woman of character and Christ-likeness. She was creative and I enjoyed being around her. "Marva will be having carryout if she doesn't get here soon" she said, and we both chuckled. As we looked up, Marva was coming across the room. "Hey yall" with her eyes beaming and that look of yall knew that I would be late so don't say nothing. Marva had a wonderful sense of humor also. We all smiled, spoke, embraced and the small talk began again as a threesome.

The waitress must have been watching us because as soon as Marva sat down she came over to take our drink order. We gave her our order and we continued to talk. We would have these soups to nuts conversations. We were really just venting and letting go. In our friendship, Marva was a source of quiet strength, the voice of reason. She made me feel like I could do just about any task that I set my mind to. She had plenty of confidence in me. I didn't know why, but it helped me to be strong. She was polished, soft-spoken and patient. I was struggling in all of those areas. In our relationship she helped me to smooth out some of the rough edges of my personality. We were traveling buddies. Together, we traveled to some of the most spectacular places in the world. You don't hang with a person like that and don't get to really know who they are. She has the gift of hospitality and giving. At the beginning of our friendship, her gentle and ladylike mannerisms made me feel awkward when in her presence. In time, she helped me to bring forth the gentler side of me. Being a Godly woman she always tried to see the positive side of things. I sometimes chuckle to myself when I think of the relationship that the three of us share. It is good to have friends to whom you are accountable. There were times when we could have been the Three Stooges, just doing silly-girly things. Other times we could have been the Three Musketeers when we had to have each other's back, stand our ground and fight. Now we are probably the Golden Girls just enjoying life as it comes. The three of us have shared some incredible, wonderful, intimate moments together. Some would say that we complemented each other because our personalities were so interchangeable. Yet we were quite different.

When the waitress came back with our drinks, we were ready to order. I was hungry and just wanted plenty of whatever I would order. Dessa got chicken, Marva got beef and I had seafood. We talked and laughed and worked on solving the problems of the world, for that day. It was good to relax, although I had a secret that I hadn't shared with my girlfriends and it stayed in the back of my mind fighting to get free.

Chapter Two

The phone was ringing off the hook, as I got out of the shower. I decided to let it ring and let the answering machine pick it up. I started to dry off and it started to ring again. I thought to myself this must be someone that really wants to talk to me. No one knew that I had taken the day off. I picked it up and said "Hello". I wished that I had let it ring when I heard who was on the other end. I knew that this call was not going to make me feel warm and fuzzy, but I engaged in conversation anyway. It was my baby's daddy, Victor. He didn't call unless he had some drama. "Hey baby, what's up?" was his usual greeting. I learned how to cut through the chase with him; too bad I didn't learn it earlier in our dating relationship. "Nothing, what do you want" I replied dryly. "You're not very talkative today, uh?" he was trying to be smart. I gave him the silent treatment. "I didn't expect you to pick up. I was going to leave you a message". I didn't respond. "Okay, well uh, I had a question. I was wondering if you were getting money from my job because they said that a lien had been put on my check for back child support". I was still silent as my mind gathered all of the things that I wanted to say to him and compiled them into a statement that would be God honoring. Our, my son was away at college. I know (@578#$) well that he ain't calling me about his job taking money from his check after all these years. Victor had been living large while I had to financially raise our, no my son alone. I really didn't need his financial support as much as I needed his moral support. If he had spent more time with him, I might be able to be more

9

forgiving, but Victor didn't even do that. Once I thought that I could answer him, without using expletives, I calmly said "No". He tried to have a conversation, but my mind closed him out as I revisited, in a flash, how I was a single parent, the struggle, and the sacrifices. The times that he couldn't be found, the many birthdays that were missed, the promises that were not kept, and the court ordered money that he did not send…. suddenly the doorbell rang. I refocused and spoke, "Okay Victor I have to go, someone is at the door". "Oh okay, just let me know when that starts so I can know where my money is going". "Okay bye", I hung up the phone and turned my attention to the ringing doorbell. I peeped out of the window and didn't recognize a car in front of my door so I thought that it was probably some Jehovah Witnesses, I didn't have time to deal with them this morning.

As I continued to get dress, I said out loud "He got some nerve!" Victor was never a good father. I got angry with myself for choosing him and angrier because I thought that I could change him. There is some truth in the statement about hindsight being twenty-twenty. How dare he call me and ask me about some damn child support (Lord forgive me), back or present! He probably was wondering why they were taking it now; our child was pretty much grown. Well, I guess that's why they call it *back* child support. He didn't pay anything when he was supposed to; he probably thought that it would just go away or that I wouldn't pursue it. He was wrong. I hope they stick it to him good. It's like the saying goes, you will either pay now or you will pay later.

That statement can be true in more ways than one. My mother warned me about Victor. She said that we were from different sides of the street. She made that statement like she was some psychic or something. Victor was a good looking guy, easy on the eyes. He had a sculptured body like a Greek god. His lips were like butter and he knew what to say out of them. He was neat and always smelled good. For a young woman entering her early twenties, that was a good start, in my thinking. He was fun to be with and he showed some interest in me. I wasn't the average girl during that time. Most guys wanted girls that were, fair skinned; skinny with wind-blowing type hair. That was the trend. I had none of that. I was flattered that he wanted to spend time with me. I didn't realize at the time that I was the prize. He won my heart and I willingly gave him the rest of me.

That was a decision that I paid for back then, but he would pay for now! I have no regrets over having my child, but if I knew then, what I know now, I would have listened to mama and not crossed the street. I would have waited and stayed on my side of the street. Humph, I probably would have gone down a different street altogether.

Clearing my head, I grabbed my car keys and headed for the door. I had more pressing things to do today than to think about Victor and his drama. I was on my way to a meeting and I didn't want to be late.

I had my "To do list" for the day. I hated to start my day off aggravated, so after I got into my car, I just sat still for a moment. I began to pray to the Lord for peace and guidance (something I should have done when my feet hit the floor, Lord, please forgive me). I didn't want to be angry with Victor. I had moved on with my life. He was just so disappointing and I was just so annoyed by his way of thinking. I took a few deep breaths, finished my prayer and started my car. It would probably take me thirty minutes to get to my meeting, so I slipped in a gospel music CD and begin to sing along like I was the artist.

Lynn had asked me to coordinate her birthday party. She wanted me to handle it from beginning to end so that meant a lot of planning. I had scheduled a meeting for the place that she wanted to have it at and was on my way to meet with the owner today.

When I got to the hall, I saw two women standing in the foyer. I assumed that one of them was Mrs. Wynfield the lady that I had spoken with on the phone. When she turned and called out my name I was surprised. She didn't look like she sounded. She was a small framed lady, dressed in ethic attire. Her hair was naturally twisted up on top of her head into an upsweep hairstyle. Her voice was very firm and direct. "Ms. Allis" she inquired as she started towards me. "Yes" I replied. "How nice to meet you, I am Mrs. Wynfield". "It's nice to meet you also". "Join me in my office" she said, as she used her hand to direct the way. Her office was neatly organized with some personal pictures and items on her desk. She had a brightly painted deep yellow accent wall behind her desk. On the wall, she had hung some beautifully framed artwork. The aroma of incense encircled the air making it kind of heavy, but pleasant. Everything had a place. I liked that. "Did you have a hard time finding us?" "Actually

I did not; you gave me very good directions". We both smiled politely and our business began.

Mrs. Wynfield was very professional and thorough. The meeting was about an hour and a half. I had enough time to do a few more things on my To do list, so I said my final thank you's and good bye's to Mrs. Wynfield and was out the door. I wanted it to be a simple but eloquent party. I knew that most of the hard work was going to be done by the caterer anyway. That was the plus of renting a nice hall. You could get the space, furnishings, the set-up and the food menu all in one. I was just providing some specialty items and planning a program for the evening. Lynn trusted me. She knew that I would make it nice, but not stiff. I believed that the party should reflect her personality. Lynn was down to earth, easy to deal with, but no pushover. She loved to laugh and listen to good music, and where there was good music Lynn would be dancing. So my hardest task was to get a good music mixologist or in simpler terms, a disc jockey. Outside the weather was warm with a slight breeze blowing and I was feeling more like myself.

I needed to go to the party warehouse to check on the prices of some items. I wasn't trying to spend a lot of money on stuff that people were just going to throw away. In my mind, I was picturing the colors that Lynn wanted to use. I sure hoped that they had everything she needed in those colors. I really didn't want to run all over town to get five things here and ten things somewhere else. I thought that I probably should have ordered all of the items from a catalog, but then I wouldn't be sure of the exact material or color blend. I was particular about those things.

Chapter Three

Whten I pulled onto the parking lot of the warehouse, it was jammed packed with cars and people. I thought they were giving something away. Fortunately, someone was getting in their car to leave a parking space as I was entering the lot. "Thank you Lord" I said to myself. I waited patiently for them to pull out so I could back in. I don't know why it takes people so long to get out of a parking space especially when they see that someone else is trying to get into it. After they pulled out, I backed into the space. I turned off my car. As I sat there watching people go back and forth, I was thinking about my plan of action. I wanted to get in and out. Prayerfully they would have everything that I needed. When I mustered up enough energy to face the crowd, I grabbed my keys, stepped out of my car and headed towards the store. There were people all over the place. The party warehouse was next door to a grocery store and I thought that maybe that was the reason as to why the parking lot was so crowded. I was right; the grocery store was having some kind of promotion and give-a-way. They had free hotdogs and juice. People could sign up to win a free car or vacation. I could have used all of the give-a-ways, but I wasn't willing to deal with the crowd. I started to turn around and get back into my car when I heard someone call my name. As I turned in the direction of the voice, I wasn't sure who the person was that was calling out my name. As she moved closer to me I realized that it was my old classmate Jeanette.

I had not seen Jeanette in over thirty years. I was surprised that she even recognized me. I was still pleasingly plump, but my hair was a little gray and longer. My skin tone had even out and my acne had cleared up. She was no longer the thin, shapely cheerleader that she was in school. I would dare say that, although I thought it. Then my mouth ran ahead of my thoughts anyway and before I could put the brakes on my tongue, I heard myself saying "Girl, I would not have known you in passing; you can wear my clothes now!" We both had a good laugh. She had put on another body. Jeanette always could laugh at herself. Even though she had the shape of a coke- a- cola bottle, in school, she struggled with a learning disability, a skin disorder and big feet. Jeanette wore a size nine shoe when most of us were wearing a size seven. We all had our crosses to bear. Now, none of that stuff mattered. We started catching up on missed time. She was married with two children, a girl and a boy. She was working for the government, FBI. She lived out in the county and life was good. Somehow, I knew that she was going to say that life was wonderful for her. She had married a guy that had a big position at IBM. Jeanette always did say that she wasn't going to work hard and that she was going to be taken care of. She said "I am now working towards full-time housewife status". We both laughed again. I wasn't really trying to claim full-time housewife status, but I certainly didn't want to work hard for much longer. We talked a little longer and I told her about my son, my job which was getting on my nerves, and a few events that had happened in my life. We exchanged telephone numbers and promised to keep in touch. After a hug, she patted me on my back and started walking towards her car. I watched her until she got lost in the crowd on the parking lot. I looked at the time. I had been talking with Jeanette for about thirty minutes, I had to get moving.

I was hoping that the party warehouse would have everything that I wanted and in the right color. I pulled out my checklist and started going up and down the aisles. There were so many choices and prices. I was on a budget and was going to try my best to stick to it. As I looked at the tableware, I saw the plates that I liked but I didn't see the color. I saw all of the other accessories, the napkins, cups and tablecloth. I thought that I was overlooking them. So I took the one that they had in blue and I went to find a salesperson to help me. I didn't know that my next fifteen minutes would mean dealing with Zora, the tattoo queen. At first, I thought that she was a customer trying to get some assistance like me. I noticed that she had a flowered tattoo leading from her neck up to the back of her ear. When she turned around I saw an earring through her nose and her employee badge. I knew then that I was in for an experience. "Excuse me" I said "Could you please tell me if you have this plate in peach?" While chewing gum and batting her false eyelashes she said unemotionally, "I'll check and see, give me a minute." I stood there thinking to myself, Lord help me not to judge what I see. She was a busty young lady and the girls were trying to get out of her blouse. Her stretch pants had reached their limit of stretch. Her pink and red hair was colored unevenly. Although the more I looked at it, the more I felt that the color pattern was intentional. She walked down the aisle before me and began to look for the plate throughout the section. When she bent over, her blouse rose up and right in the center of her back was another tattoo of a rose. "I don't see it out here". I thought in silence, well I could have told you that. That is why I came to you. "Do you know if it comes in peach?" "I'm not sure, I don't see it" she said. I took a deep breath and asked, "Can you check to see if this particular plate does come in peach and if so, do you have any in stock? I do see that it comes in some other colors. I continued making my request, if it does come in peach, and you don't have it in stock, I would like to order it." I thought that I had made myself clear. "I don't see any peach out here" she repeated herself. I could feel my facial muscles tighten. My half smile began to firm up. My tone was different as my request became more of a directive. "Would you please check?" She probably sensed the irritation in my tone, so without even looking at me she said "Okay, I'll go check". I wanted to sarcastically say, yeah do that! But instead I just said "thank you" through my clenched teeth. The Lord is still working with me on my patience.

As I stood there at the counter waiting for Zora the tattoo queen to return, I began to focus on the rest of my day. Mae, Dee and I had planned to go to the movies. I hadn't told them my secret yet. I didn't like keeping things from them, but I had to get comfortable with the information myself. "We do have them in peach" I heard the sales girl say with a little more enthusiasm than before. If you give me a few minutes I will get someone to get them from stock for you, okay?" I nodded in agreement, halfway still stuck in my thoughts about how I wanted to share my information with my girlfriends. Things were changing for me.

I had some mixed feelings and concerns about all the details. I didn't want to make a mistake this far into my life. God had been good to me. I had always been independent and managed my life pretty well with his guidance.

A balloon burst and the sound brought me back to where I was. The young man brought me the plates and I got the rest of the accessories that I needed to go with them. I paid Zora for my items and left the store. People were still coming and going on the parking lot. I got to my car, placed my purchases into the back and climbed into the driver's seat. I saw that someone was waiting to get into my space, so I started the car and pulled out of the space. I didn't want to be one of those persons that sat in a parking space knowing that someone else was waiting to get into it. That annoyed me to no end. After checking my list, I got almost everything I needed at the party warehouse in one trip. I was glad about that. Now it was on to the next thing on my To Do list.

I stopped past the post office to get some stamps. Then I went to Wal-Mart to get the rest of the items on my list. Wal-Mart was always busy and I always ran into someone I knew. I was praying that today would not be one of those days. I finished my errands and was looking forward to getting home to take a nap before I went out tonight.

Chapter Four

I grabbed my mail out of the mailbox before I went into the house. I laid it on the dining room table but noticed a brightly colored envelope mixed in with the rest of the mail. As I put down the other bags that I had in my hands, I saw that the message light was blinking on the phone. I went to the refrigerator to get some water. I had to make myself drink water. I hadn't drunk any today and it was three-thirty already. I sipped a little from the bottle and chewed on a piece of cheese. I sat down at the table to relax for a while. My eyes fell on my mail and I reached for the brightly colored envelope first. It looked like an invitation of some sort. Invitations usually meant that I had to spend some money. It was nicely handwritten and addressed to the Occupant. A handwritten envelope isn't something that you see much of these days. I turned it over and held it up towards the light. It was a nice thick envelope, the kind that you couldn't see through, but it had no return address on it. I don't know why I was delaying opening it; after all I was the Occupant. This must be some kind of advertisement, I thought to myself. When I began to open it I could smell the inviting scent of a man's cologne. I was very curious now. Someone had gone through a lot of trouble for this to be just a gad. I eagerly ripped the envelope open and pulled out the card. It simply said "You are special". It had a little red heart with the word Jesus printed where the signature would be. There wasn't a name attached to it but I was really hoping that it was from Kevin. I quickly erased that thought because I hadn't given him my address or phone number.

Kevin seemed like a gentleman. He stood about six feet two inches tall. If I had to guess he probably weighed between one hundred eighty to one hundred ninety pounds. He looked to be very conscious of his body. He probably was the kind that ran a few miles every day. His complexion was like smooth rich mocha chocolate. His teeth were pearly white and almost perfect. His voice was as smooth as silk. Kevin could think and speak in whole sentences. He could actually hold a conversation on just about anything. I was impressed. Kevin worked for the Federal Government and did a lot of traveling (I found that out during our first conversation). This was the kind of thing that he would do. I sniffed the card and I reminisced about how we met.

I met Kevin about three months ago at my girlfriend Lynn's church. They were having a three night revival and she wanted me to come and hear the revivalist. I said that I would. He was from North Carolina. She was so excited about his preaching and singing. I don't know why people think that all preachers from North Carolina can preach. I was exhausted. My feet were swollen, my back was hurting and all I wanted to do was get a hot shower and crawl into bed. It had been a long, busy week for me. I normally would have gone earlier in the week but here it was Friday, the last night, and I knew that the church would be packed and I was right. You know how we do. We wait until the last minute, the last day the last something and then when we don't have any other choice we respond. Well, this seemed to be one of those times for a whole lot of people.

When I arrived, I really wanted to sit in the back of the church so that I could sneak out right after the preacher preached. Just as I saw what I thought was an ideal seat, the usher touched me and directed me to another seat. "Those seats are reserved for the ushers' sugar, but I have another one right up here" she had her hand out directing the way. Out of obedience I followed her lead. She sat me down right next to a nice looking man. He smiled as I took my seat on the pew. I wondered why this prime seat hadn't been taken. Then I discovered that there were children on the pew. Now, I don't have anything against children, they have to sit somewhere too. However, I don't necessarily want to be on the same pew with them if every ten minutes they have to go to the restroom. People were singing and shouting and praising the Lord. It was getting hot and the music was getting loud. The children on the pew had crossed us about three times. My facial expressions were changing every time they came my way. Suddenly, this man leaned over to me and asked "Do you belong to this church?" "I said with a slight grin "No, and I take it that you don't either. "Right, I was invited" he whispered "I hope that by the end of the service I won't have regrets." My tongue quickly spoke what my brain was thinking, "If you don't, I probably will have enough regrets for the both of us." We both gave a slight chuckle and refocused on worship.

I was excited about meeting a man that was not ashamed of being known as a Christian. Shucks, just meeting a real man would have been okay. That night he was clapping his hands and saying Amen to the preached word. I watched him from the side of my eyes. He had his bible opened and was taking notes. I checked out his fingers to see if there was a ring, there wasn't. That doesn't mean anything, but I was curious. He made me feel comfortable as we sat together on the pew praising the Lord.

When service was over, some people began to shake hands and give each other hugs. Some people were talking and kissing each other on the cheeks. I was trying to make my way out of the door, I was already tired. My pew partner touched me on the arm and said "Are you traveling by yourself? Do you need someone to walk you to your car?" "Not really, I said "I do this all the time" "Not in this neighborhood you do, let me walk with you" he said slightly smiling. I turned and said "Alright". As we made our way to the exit, I caught my co-worker's eye. With one finger in the air, she was beckoning for me to wait a minute for her. I knew that it would be rude to just leave especially now that she saw me. I told my pew partner that my co-worker wanted to speak to me so if he wanted to go ahead that it would be okay. "Oh no, it's no problem. I can wait for you. He leaned closer and whispered in my ear "remember the kind of neighborhood that you are in and the time of night it is". I smiled. Her church didn't have a security ministry like my church. I stood aside the wall as she made her way to me. She gave me a big hug while she shouted with excitement "I'm glad that you came, wasn't that an awesome word?" I simply said I was encouraged. "He is such a great preacher, he comes every year" she must have noticed that my pew partner was standing rather close to me; she paused and gave him a glance. Noticing her expression I said "I'm sorry, Lynn this is …..... Kevin "he said as he stretched out his hand to shake hers. "Oh, nice to meet you", I didn't know that you were bringing someone with you. "Actually, I met Kevin here, he was visiting too". "Oh, really "she said looking at him like he was a biscuit and she was the jelly, "Did someone invite you? " My neighbor, Ms. Ida Mae Johnson, he said. "Oh, I know Sister Johnson, does she know that you are here?" "No, but I will inform her of my visit when I see her" Kevin said with the tone of because right now I am leaving. I was beginning to like this guy. "I was just going to make sure that … he suddenly turned to me and realized that he hadn't asked me my name. "Sandy" I replied quickly as to not to leave him hanging, and we both laughed out loud". He completed his statement, "I was just about to walk Sandy to her car to make sure that she got off safely". "Oh, such a gentleman" Lynn said scanning him from head to toe. As not to hold Kevin up any longer, I quickly said "Okay girl, thanks for inviting me, we will talk later, Love Ya." I gave her a big hug and kiss on her cheek and turned to join Kevin as we continued to make our way through the crowd.

Outside he asked me where I had parked. I pointed and said, "Right up the street near the corner". We started walking in that direction. In my mind I started having some reality thoughts, now I don't really know this man and here I am allowing him to walk me to my car in this neighborhood. I knew that everybody sitting up in church wasn't necessarily a practicing Christian. I hadn't parked too far away, even though I was running late when I got there. Some other people from the church were walking behind us, so I didn't feel too bad. At least they could hear my cry for help if I needed to holler out. Whew, my imagination was running wild! I had to come back to the moment. Kevin broke the silence when he asked me "So where do you go to church since this is not your home church?' I took a deep breath and said "If I tell you will you come and visit?" "Sure, I am currently looking for a place of worship". "I belong to Morning Glory Baptist Church", I said proudly. "I've heard of that church. I've only been living here for about three months. I travel a lot for my job. I work for the Federal government" he injected. "I think that's the church that I have seen on TV". "Well, you can come and visit us and see if it is a place where you may want to worship on a regular basis."

I was at my car, so I stopped and said "This is my car, thanks for caring enough about my safety to walk me to it." "Not a problem, I wouldn't want anything to happen to my sister in Christ. He waited until I got inside and started it up. I opened the window a little to say thank you again and good night. He smiled a big wide smile and said "My pleasure, maybe I'll see you again". I pulled off slowly and he turned to go back down the street. I wanted to offer him a ride back to his car, mainly because I wanted to see what he was driving. As I watched him disappear into the darkness of the night through my rear view mirror, I turned the corner and started home.

I sniffed the brightly colored envelope once again. I released my thoughts about Kevin from pause and I smiled. Remembering him made me feel good on the inside. I turned to look out of the kitchen window and the blinking light on the phone caught my attention. I pushed the button to see that I had four new messages. I let them play while I got some water from the refrigerator. They were from my sister, my doctor, my co-worker and then a mysterious message. I played the mysterious message a few times but didn't recognize the man's voice. The message simply said that they had been trying to reach me and hoped to do so soon. I checked the caller ID and it wasn't a number that I was familiar with. I was puzzled, so I called the number back but all I got was a recording that said that the number that I was trying to reach didn't accept incoming calls. I was baffled, who could this be. I thought about Kevin again, but how would he have gotten my information. Maybe the envelope and the phone call had nothing to do with each other. Although in my mind, I sensed that they did. I finish drinking my water and put the phone call out of my mind for the time being.

Chapter Five

I went upstairs to get me a nap before I got ready to go out to the movies with the girls. It felt good to lie across the bed and close my eyes. In my mind I replayed the day's events. I had covered a lot of ground, but still had a lot to do. This felt like a work day even though I had taken the day off. As I cleared my mind I slowly drifted off to sleep.

The ringing of the phone startled me. I reached for it half asleep. It was Dessa on the other end. "Hey girl, did I wake you?" she said. "Yeah, I was trying to catch a little nap before we went to the movie. Are we still on for the same time?" "Yeah, that is good for me" she said quickly. "Okay that gives me about one hour to get ready. Can you check with Marva and have her just meet us there?" I asked. "Okay, I can do that. Can you pick me up?" she asked. "Yeah, that will not be a problem" I replied.

I hung up the phone, turned over onto my back and looked at the ceiling. I really wanted to get up, take a shower and get back into the bed. Lately, my energy level seemed really low. Just about every day now, I had to talk myself into going to work. It had gotten to the point that I had to talk myself into going anywhere. It wasn't that I didn't want to go; I just didn't want to do the preliminaries that were required before I got out of the door. I didn't know what was wrong with me. I lay still for a few more minutes and then I talked myself into getting up to take a quick shower.

I got out of the shower, dried off and put some lotion on, my skin was so dry. I felt a little better. My mind went back to that mysterious phone call. It didn't sound threatening, and the messenger spoke as though I

23

would know who it was. I looked at the clock; I needed to pick up Dessa in about fifteen minutes in order to get to the movie on time. I checked myself out in the mirror, everything looked good, and I was halfway downstairs when I realized that I had left my pocketbook in my room on the dresser. I turned around to go back up the stairs and the phone rang. "Who is that?" I said out loud debating in my mind whether or not to answer it. I was pressed for time so I really didn't want to engage in a conversation with someone that had some drama. So I decided not to answer it. I just grabbed my purse and headed for the door. I didn't want to be late for the beginning of the movie.

When I pulled up in front of Dessa's house her front door was open. That was a sign that she was ready and nearby. Nobody is walking around leaving their doors open and unlocked these days. She probably left it open so she could see me pull up. I had picked her up so many times before for one thing or another that I knew the routine. It wasn't that Dessa didn't like driving, but if she moved her car on her block and stayed out too late, it was likely that she wouldn't have a parking space close to her door when she got back. No woman in her right mind would be walking around in Dessa's neighborhood by herself late at night. Parking was a problem on my street too, but I had a parking pad in my back yard. I didn't sit long before Dessa came through the door carrying her purse over her shoulder. She walked around the front of the car and opened the door. "Hey girl" she said as she crawled into the passenger side. "I almost forgot the passes. I had to run back upstairs to get them. How are you doing? "I'm fine as she leaned over to greet me with a hug. Dessa always had a coupon, card or pass for something. She didn't mind sharing her goodies with her girlfriends. "You didn't call me did you?" "No, I was trying to find something to wear that I could be comfortable in". "I know that's right. I hope that this is a good movie. Did you get Marva?" I asked. "Yeah, she said that she would meet us in front of the movie. I told her that I had passes and if she was late then we would leave her pass at the box office, but that we would save her a seat." We laughed, but we both knew that that would probably be the case. At least this way all of us wouldn't miss the beginning of the movie.

We found a parking space right in front of the door. "Great!" I said with excitement. Dessa gave me a high five and we made our way out of the car and into the theatre. Much to our surprise, Marva was standing on the inside of the lobby. "How long have you been here?" Dessa asked her with surprise in her voice. "What do you mean, you act like I can't get nowhere on time!" she said jokingly. "You can't" Dessa and I said in unison and then we all started laughing out loud. We sometimes had to remember where we were when we got together. We were like high school girls acting silly and just being ourselves. We gave her a hug and went to give the usher our passes.

The theatre was packed, but we were lucky; there were three seats together on a row. It was if they were waiting just for us to claim them, so we did. After excusing ourselves as we crossed the couple on the end, we were able to reach our seats and settle in. The movie hadn't started yet so we quietly chatted about our day. For a moment, my mind drifted to the secret that I was holding in my heart. I knew that I wanted to tell my girlfriends about it, but this wasn't the time to do it. So I took a deep breath and refocused on our present conversation.

The lights began to dim and the movie began. I really tried to enjoy the movie, but my thoughts were somewhere else. I was still puzzled about that mysterious phone call that I received and the secret that I was holding back from Dessa and Marva. I knew that I had to pull it together or eventually they would be able to tell that something was wrong. I never could disguise my feelings. They always showed on my face and in my behavior.

When the movie was over, like three blind mice, we made our way out into the lobby. "Are we going to get something to eat?" That was Marva's favorite phrase. "Okay. What is around here?" Dessa asked. "We can walk across and down the street to the Little Big Appetite Restaurant, Marva said. "Is that okay with you Sandy?" "That's fine; I probably will just have a salad". Marva continued by telling us that the restaurant had really good food and an inviting atmosphere. The truth of the matter was that it really wasn't about the food; we just enjoyed each other's company. Although having a good meal on the side was a plus.

When we stepped into the restaurant, I checked out the décor. It was nicely furnished with private booths and dim lights hanging from the ceiling. In the center of each table was a little flower arrangement that added a special touch. It was cozy. On many occasions when I went out to eat, I always ran into someone that I knew, an old classmate, a former student, or a church member. This time it was Dessa that ran into an old friend. We were seated at a booth midway the restaurant. The sounds of the restaurant were lively and filled with conversation and laughter. Suddenly I saw a lady approaching the table. She stopped at the table and said "Dessa, I thought that was you. I saw you when you came in and I said to my friend, I know that lady". Dessa looked up and a wide grin creeped across her face. "Sylvia? Girl it has been years!" They both laughed out loud as Dessa got up to embrace her. Almost in unison they asked each other how they had been. Sylvia was a tall, big boned, but well-proportioned lady with a deep chocolate complexion. She wore her hair in a natural hairstyle and had a hearty laugh. They broke conversation long enough for Dessa to introduce us. "Sylvia, I want you to meet my two girlfriends, Sandy and Marva ". "Hi, how are you?" we both said together. "I'm just fine, good to meet you both. Dessa and I go way back. I use to live right up the street from her on Beach Street. We had some really good times when we were growing up as neighbors." They went on to exchange a few more pleasantries and then she turned and said "Yall enjoy your meal. Dessa now you have my number so keep in touch with me". "Okay, I will. Take care of yourself" Dessa replied. As Dessa sat back down she could hardly wait to tell us that Sylvia use to be a piece of work. Dessa laughed when she told us the story of Sylvia and her first real boyfriend and how she found out that he was seeing another girl at the same time that he was seeing her. "Boy did she put a hurting on him" Dessa remembered. "Sylvia would fight at the drop of a hat". She had five brothers and she was the only girl, yeah she had something for you if you crossed her" Dessa recounted. For a moment it was like she was back on Beach Street. When the waitress came to our table Dessa returned to the present with the words, "Those were the days". The waitress took our order and we sat and discussed the movie and our day. After we ate, we paid the check and gathered our belongings to go home. We walked back to our cars laughing and talking. When we got to Marva's car, we hugged each other good night and Dessa and I walked down a few more cars to get into my car. It had been a good evening but I was tired and kind of glad to be going home. Dessa and I chattered all the way to her house. Then just before she got out of the car she turned to me and said "Get some rest, you look tired. I noticed that you were moving like you were in pain throughout the night, is everything okay?" I was caught off guard with her question, but I just said "Yeah, I am a little tired it has been a busy day". She said "Okay I love you, call me when you get in so that I will know that you made it in alright". "Okay, I love you too". I watched her as she made her way into her house and then I drove off.

On the drive home I thought about how I was going to tell Dessa and Marva that I was…oh well, I didn't have to think about that right now. I was more concerned about that mysterious phone call and card. My life suddenly had some loose ends that I desperately wanted to tie up and get rid of.

Chapter Six

Traffic was awful going into work today. I heard on the radio that there was an accident on the interstate and cars were taking the exit that led to the street that I normally took to work. That just made all the side streets backed up with traffic. People were cutting off other drivers and breaking all the rules of the road. It made for a hectic morning commute and patience seemed to be in short supply as drivers tempers flared. I just wanted to get to my job without having an accident.

When I pulled onto the parking lot, my nemesis, Mrs. Eastman, was pulling in at the same time. I really didn't feel like any drama from her today. I had already pressed my way through a maze of side streets to get here. So I just sat in my car for a few moments until she went into the building. I figured that if I gave her a head start then she would be in her room by the time that I entered the building. I thought to myself, as I looked up to the partly cloudy sky, I probably should have called out today. I suddenly felt like I wanted to be at home watching a movie and sipping on a nice hot cup of herbal tea. When I thought that I had given her enough time to get to her room, I got out of my car and started for the door. There wasn't anyone in the halls. "Good" I said to myself, "maybe I can make it to my office before I ran into someone that wanted to have a long conversation. I just didn't feel like it today. When I entered the office I heard Mrs. Eastman's voice. "Shoot" I said to myself. She was in someone else's office giving them grief. I could tell from the tone that something was up. I really didn't care. I signed in and made my way to my office and shut the door.

It was halfway through the day when I looked up at my office clock. I had managed to get a lot of things done without the usual interruptions. I was just about to open my office door to take a break and get a breath of fresh air when I heard Mrs. Eastman. I thought to myself, maybe I will wait until she goes pass my door before I open it. I was frozen to my chair, praying that she wasn't coming to my office. She always brings drama, has a problem or wants to get something stirred up. Her knock at my door sounded like one of the three. I hesitated to move towards it. I started not to answer it when I heard another voice along with hers. When I moved to the door I could hear myself say out loud "Lord help me be at peace". When I opened the door Mrs. Eastman and Mrs. Martin, the district supervisor, were standing side by side. Both of them had anxious looks on their faces. I knew in my spirit that Mrs. Martin had been summoned. She hardly ever came to my office unless there was a problem. "Hi," I said with a superficial smile on my face. "What brings you to my neck of the woods? Come on in. I was just getting ready to go to lunch." "Okay, then I won't hold you. I just wanted you to pull an invoice for me. There seems to be a discrepancy about an order that Mrs. Eastman placed and has not received. Mrs. Martin looked at me with the look of, would you please just pacify me with this. I understood the look because Mrs. Eastman gets on everyone's nerves. The sheer fact that Mrs. Martin was there told me that she had run to her about the supply order issue that I told her I would get back to her on. I had located the invoice, did some checking and found out what the problem was. I just had not had the time to get back to Mrs. Eastman. I had other things on my mind and it really wasn't a matter of urgency. I turned to Mrs. Eastman and said, "Is this about the invoice that we spoke about on the other day or so?" "Yes", she said in a snippy tone. "I need those supplies and you haven't said a word about them. I know that I ordered them for my area and you just went on and gave them to Mrs. Hillery". "That is not what happened Mrs. Eastman" I was calm in my response. "I told you that I would check the invoice to see if there was some kind of mix up or something, and I did. "Thank you, Mrs. Allis" Mrs. Martin injected as to defuse any more comments that may be on the tip of Mrs. Eastman's tongue. "That sure does save me a lot of work.

We have so many of these invoices that come through the area office that we have to depend on the site supervisors to keep them straight". I knew that if anybody knew what happened with the supplies you would. "So what did you find", she said without even so much as a glance in Mrs. Eastman's direction. "Well, because Mrs. Eastman and Mrs. Hillery had ordered some of the same items the company put them on the same invoice so that we could get a better deal price wise. They shipped them together but according to the amount ordered on the invoice. So now all they have to do is separate the order according to their personal requisition. None of the boxes have been opened because I wanted to have the requisitions and the invoices in front of me to compare." Mrs. Martin nodded her head okay and said, "That makes sense and that should resolve this issue." Mrs. Eastman was still not happy. I knew that she would not be. She was looking for a fight and some kind of reprimand of me. She didn't get it, and she wasn't happy. I on the other hand was pleased as could be. Mrs. Martin was a full-full figured woman. She had a lot of experience with the likes of Mrs. Eastman. After a few more verbal exchanges she said "Well, Ms. Allis thank you for your time. I have some further business with Mrs. Eastman so we are going to her area to finish up". Mrs. Eastman looked like a balloon that was ready to pop. She could hardly wait to push her way through my office door into the hall. Mrs. Martin turned to me when she got to the door and whispered, "She is a piece of work, isn't she?" We both smiled in agreement.

I decided to go out of the building for lunch. I grabbed my purse and started towards the door when my cell phone started to ring. I reached in my purse and looked at the number. I didn't recognize the number, nor did I? For some reason it did look familiar. Then I remembered that it was the same number that I saw on my caller ID. I checked to see if they had left a message. It was the same voice, but this time it seemed more familiar. It said "I'm sorry I missed you, but I hope to see you soon". This was scary but in a weird way exciting.

Very few people had my cell phone number because I was not really a cell phone user. Most people kept their cell phones attached to their hip. I rarely used mine unless I was out of town or had an emergency. I was just getting comfortable with the technology of the answering machine; whereby people could call and leave a message even when you weren't home. Now with the use of the cell phone people could call you no matter where you were. Used improperly, that was too much invasion of privacy for me. I liked to control my own time and space. People who really wanted to take some time and have a casual conversation with me would call me at home. So I felt like this wasn't a matter of importance.

I sat in my car and listened to the message again. It was beginning to sound more and more like Kevin, but I wasn't sure. When I remembered the sound of his voice in my mind, he had the same smoothness in his voice. I just didn't know how he could have gotten my information. I remembered that he told me that he worked for the federal government. I don't think he mentioned the agency. If he had said the FBI or the CIA, I probably would have remembered that. I didn't commit much of his information to mind because I really didn't think that I would ever see him again.

I went and got my lunch, ate it on the run as usual, and tried to finish my day without incident. I worked in my office for the rest of the day purposely avoiding any contact with Mrs. Eastman. At the end of the day, I organized my desk and left a note for myself to remind me of what would need my immediate attention on tomorrow. I sat at my desk for a few moments. I whispered a prayer. It had been a mentally stressful day. I had some big decisions to make. I was dealing with my job and my personal life. I had been praying and asking the Lord for guidance. I didn't want to move to fast, but Lord knows I needed to do something about my situation. One thing for sure, I needed to find a way to tell my two best girlfriends what was going on with me personally. I had mixed emotions and didn't understand why I was so hesitant about telling them. They had always been so supportive of me, but this matter was hard for me to deal with. I felt that it might really test the strength of our friendship. I had so much to do in the coming weeks. I wasn't ready to put my secret out there to have to deal with it along with everything else. One day, one situation at a time. That is all I had energy for right now. I needed to stop pass Lynn's house to show her what I had picked up for her birthday party that I was coordinating. Lynn lived all the way across town. In my spirit I cried out for the Lord to give me strength!

I called Lynn before I left the parking lot. "Hello, Lynn?" I said in an unsure kind of way. "Hey Ally" she answered in a soft mysterious kind of tone. Most people called me Sandy; Lynn liked to call me Ally putting a twist on my last name. I didn't mind. Lynn was usually so upbeat when she answered her phone, I wasn't sure that I had dialed the right number. "What's up? Is everything okay?" I asked cautiously. She slowly replied "Yeah, I was sitting on the porch drifting in and out of sleep". "Okay, I was going to come by and show you what I picked up at the store for your party. Is that okay?" I asked. "Oh yeah, that's fine" she said sounding more like herself "come on over, I will be here".

As I pulled up in front of Lynn's house she was sitting on the porch. She immediately recognized my car and started waving. Lynn was a lively soul. She had a way of making you feel right at home. I needed her warmth. She came to the car and gave me a great big old hug and started in with the conversation. "I was glad that you called. I was sitting here on this porch, just as tired as I could be, when the phone rang. I started not to answer it. I can hardly get a moment's peace before somebody, somewhere think that they have to call and give me something to do!" She was almost out of breath, but didn't stop. "I tell you, girl this party is about to drive me insane. People want to show up when they want to, bring who they want and all kinds of crazy stuff. I almost want to call it off. You know that I don't have much tolerance for foolishness". "Well, Lynn", I said in a calm voice, "I still have my receipts". We both paused and caught each other's eyes, and then we both laughed. "Girl you know that I am just blowing off steam. I am looking forward to my birthday celebration. I am not going to let them get on my nerves but so much" she said. We continued to laugh and talk as we removed the bags from the trunk of the car and took them into her house.

You have done some things to the house since I've been here. "Yeah girl, when was the last time that you were here? It had to have been over a year" she said without giving me a chance to answer. "I had to get new windows. I put on a front door, laid down new wood floors in the dining and living room. Brought some new appliances for the kitchen, painted, whew! I have almost rebuilt this place. "Well it really does look good. " I said as she took a breath. "A woman's got to do what a woman's got to do" she chuckled as she began to take items from the bag. "How are things with you?" Have you seen that fine guy that I saw you with at church? I saw Sis. Ida Mae Johnson, I started to ask her about him. He certainly was a tall drink of water". Lynn was a talker. She could engage you in other conversations for hours if you let her. Tonight I wasn't feeling it. I redirected her attention to the purpose of my visit. "So, how do you like all of the colored coordinated plates, cups and napkins?" I asked. "I love them. I knew that you would make sure that everything matched. I wasn't worried about what you would buy. I trust your judgment. Just give me the receipts". She went back to her former statement like we hadn't moved on. "You know what, come to think about it, I remember Ms. Ida Mae asking the church to pray for one of her neighbors. She said that he was a fine young man. Of course she meant fine as in decent, upright kind of guy. I wondered if she was talking about him. What was his name?" "Kevin", I said softly. "Yeah that's right, that's the name she called him. That was about three weeks ago". I thought to myself, maybe he was still in town. Maybe it was him that sent me that mysterious card and has been leaving those messages on my phone. A girl can wish can't she?

Lynn and I talked and laughed about a little bit of everything, although I didn't plan to stay as long as I did. Lynn had a way of lifting my spirits and making me realize that things weren't as bad as they seemed. When I looked at the clock, it was late. I told her that I had to go but would call her on tomorrow. We hugged and said our good-byes. She watched me get into my car and pull off.

As I started my journey home I knew that I needed to clear my mind of all the things that had happened this day. I started thinking about my job, the people on it and retirement. I was so tired of the petty politics on the job. Every day it was something new to see if my blood pressure could go up any higher. One thing I didn't want to do was die on the job. I realized that I needed to start thinking about some changes in my life. But for right now all I wanted to do was to just get home, take my shower and go straight to bed. Somehow in my spirit I felt like that wasn't going to happen.

Chapter Seven

The alarm clock didn't go off. I had tossed and turned all night. I looked over at the clock. I was late. I laid there and stared at the ceiling. I didn't feel like rushing. My body wasn't cooperating and my mind embraced the physical feeling that I was having and before I knew it I didn't feel like going in at all. I turned over and reached for the phone to call in. I stopped and began to pray. I wasn't up for giving a detailed explanation to Mrs. Sherrod, our meddlesome secretary. One would think that she had to approve the leave. She thought that she needed to have all the details before she documented your request. She wanted to know if you were going to the doctor, what was your diagnosis and how long were you going to be out. As the phone rang, I prepared myself for cutting through the chase and only sharing the facts. I was not coming in, period. When Mrs. Hines, the office assistant picked up, I was surprised. I asked her how she was doing and then informed her that I was not coming in. She said that she would write it in the book, and that was that. Thank you Lord for answered prayer!

I stayed in bed a little longer. To my surprise I drifted off back to sleep. When I woke up it was mid-morning. I felt so much better. I didn't realize just how tired my body was. It was in complete shutdown mode. I got up and went into the bathroom. I looked at myself in the mirror. I thought to myself, "Girl you need a complete make-over, a picker-upper". I decided right then and there that since I had taken the day off, I was going to spend it on me. I turned on the shower and adjusted the temperature of the water.

I wanted this shower to be slightly cool. I stepped into the steady stream of water and just stood there. The water seemed to be rinsing away all of the concerns that I had been carrying around for the week. As I enjoyed the steady stream of refreshing water I begin to just talk to the Lord. I had a lot of things going on right now.

After I stepped out of the shower, I thought about my plans. Today I was going to the spa to get a facial, manicure and pedicure. I wanted to have my hair shampooed and conditioned and then my eyebrows arched. I might go to the mall and look around for a while and see if anything was on sale or called out my name to be bought. Then I would spend some time with my girlfriends. That sounded like a good plan. I made up my mind that this weekend I would do the hard thing, and tell Dessa and Marva about the secret that I had been carrying around with me for the past few months. Yep, that was my plan, but I was trusting that the Lord would adjust them as needed.

As I was putting on my clothes I was organizing my thoughts in my mind. I was ready to move forward. I went to the kitchen to get some juice from the refrigerator. I went to the window and pulled back the curtains to let in some sunlight. The phone rang and instinctively I picked it up. Immediately I thought to myself that I should have just let it rang. It was in my hand now so I said "Hello" cautiously. The voice on the other end of the phone said "Hello Cas-san-dra". I remembered that was the name that my father wanted to give me, but my mother changed it to her liking. Who could this be? No one ever called me Cassandra. The voice spoke it as if he was unsure of it. I was curious as to who this mysterious caller was so I said "Who do you want to speak to?" hesitantly. I wanted the voice on the other end to say more. I knew it had to be someone that thought they knew me, but wasn't really sure. The man on the other end had a deep, distinguished voice. It sort of reminded me of a radio announcer or someone. "I hope that you don't mind me calling like this. "Who is this?" I said in a more demanding tone. The voice repeated himself, "Are you Cassandra, I would like to speak to Cassandra". "I'm sorry; I didn't catch your name. Who's calling?" I asked very directly. After a few seconds he said "Herman". There was a pause. That was my father's name. Could this be a coincidence? Then he continued to speak, "Are you Cassandra? " I couldn't stop my lips from saying yes. "Well I don't know how to say this". I managed to bring some words to my mouth while my thoughts were scattered. "Excuse me, did you say Herman?" I said in disbelief as I cut across his statement. My heart stopped but my mind raced ahead. I knew that I had been searching for my father through social network, legal records, relatives, internet and other means. Could this be his voice on the other end of my phone? Maybe it was someone that knew I was looking for my father and was calling to give me some information, a lawyer maybe. The man on the other end repeated, "My name is Herman. I don't know how to tell you this except to just tell you". He paused again. I could hear him take a deep breath, "I believe that I am your father". I couldn't believe my ears. There was dead silence. Then the man chuckled nervously and said, "I know that this must be quite a surprise for you. You see, I have been trying to locate my daughter. I lost track of her some years ago. I was notified by the Drake Location Agency that you fit the background information that I had given them". I was shocked and curious at the same time. I wanted to say to him, I've been looking for you also. The caller continued to speak. "I didn't want to do this on the phone, but I thought it would be better than just walking up on you in the street or coming to your job. I had just about given up hope. I am here in town visiting and would love to meet you somewhere to talk". "How did you get my telephone number?" I began my interrogation. "How do I know that you are who you say that you are? There are a lot of quacks out there! How did you know that I would be home today? He began to explain, but I had questions that took me to another place and time blocking out his responses. I heard him talking, but I hadn't gotten past his admittance of him claiming to be my father. When the fog began to clear, he was ending with "So if it's alright with you, let's get together and make our meeting official and I will answer all the questions that I can.

Suddenly, I was more curious about the man that I had never met. Part of me wanted to meet him and ask the hard questions. The why questions, why did you leave, why didn't you check on me, why….. Yet the other part of me just wanted to see him face to face to see what he looked like and to validate who I was. Meeting him would bring closure to other areas of my life that I hadn't put periods in. The fog was completely clear now. I snapped back to the present and said, "Why don't you give me your information. You seem to have all of mine'. He laughed out loud. "Smart girl, I know that this is a lot to digest. I wouldn't expect that you would just jump up and run to meet me without some thought".

I wrote down his information and ended the phone call by letting him know that I would be getting back in touch with him real soon. I slowly released the phone from my hand making the disconnection a reality.

I was frozen in place when I hung up the phone. All of my life I had wondered about the man that was my natural father, but not consumed by the thoughts. I had so many questions swirling around in my head; I had to sit down for a few minutes. Those minutes turned into a few hours. When I went to get up, my thoughts had me paralyzed. The words of our conversation would not let me think of much else. I had to get myself together. I thought to myself, was this the Lord's way of adjusting my plans, for today? for my life? I knew that I would really have to pray about my next moves, but first I had to find enough strength to get up out of the chair.

Chapter Eight

I moved to the edge of the chair, knees bent and arms by my side, I pushed myself up to my feet. I stood there motionless for a while. What I thought would be the revealing of a secret quest was now a possible reality. My big secret had been unveiled sooner than I thought. I wanted to tell Mae and Dee that I was embarking on this quest to locate my biological father, but now I may have to tell them that I found him. Wow! I thought at first that the quest would be unproductive and even childish. After all these years one would think who cares about who he was. I thought that they would feel that I needed to get beyond it, I was grown now. I never really talked about my father, so for them it was a mute subject. They would probably be surprised that I would even initiate a search for him. I usually spoke about my stepfather when we talked about fathers. This probably wouldn't be earth shattering news for them, but I knew that they would most likely have a lot of questions. I needed to have the answers for myself before I divulged this information to them or anyone else.

I wrote the number down twice, once on the pad that I kept by the phone and then again on a piece of paper that I shoved down into the pocket of my tight jeans. I had to refocus and get moving. I really wanted to call someone to tell them what had just happened but I hadn't completely wrapped my mind around it yet. It was a lot to take in. However, I wasn't going to get anything done standing in the middle of the floor. I shook my head, grabbed my jacket from the closet and headed for the door. I know that I warmed my car up for one half hour just sitting in it while my thoughts were all over the place. "Okay girl you have got to concentrate" I said to myself. I just bowed my head and lifted up a prayer to God. I needed his direction and peace right now. I finished my prayer, put the car in drive, pulled out of my parking space and started for the spa.

I pulled into a parking space in front of the Total Spa Lady Salon and Gym. Thoughts were still twirling around in my head. How did he get my phone number? How did he even know that I would be home today? He was probably just taking his chances. I had to tell someone before I exploded. I reached for my phone to call Marva. I noticed that I had missed a call. It was Lynn. I begin to listen to her message, "Sandy, call me. You know that guy you met at church during the revival named Kevin; well Ms. Ida Mae brought him and his Hershey Chocolate father to church the other night. His father looks just as good as he does. Call me girl?" I chuckled to myself. Lynn had a thing for dark complexion men. I would call her back later; right now I needed to unwind at the spa.

As I went through my routine of thirty minutes on the exercise bike and the weights, I decided that I would end my workout with a massage, pedicure and manicure. I would skip the facial and the hair stuff. I wore my hair natural. I knew that they really didn't know what to do with natural hair. I was glad this was a full-service salon and spa. I didn't have to go anywhere else for my beauty services. They had a shower and a sauna. I took a quick shower before I checked in and went to the massage room area. I changed into the soft warm terry cloth robe that they provided; along with the terry cloth slippers. I went to sit in the waiting area waiting for them to call my name. As I reached for a magazine, a big boned woman with red colored hair and a foreign accent came to the door and called my name. She introduced herself and escorted me into the massage room. Her voice was softer than her look. The room was dimly lit and very aromatic. I looked around the space and saw bottles of lotions and ointments on the shelves. White towels were stacked up neatly at her reach. She helped me onto the table and started with a few questions. "I see that you want a full body massage. "Is that correct?" "Yes" I said. "Okay, lay face down and just relax. This will probably take about thirty-five minutes". As I lay on the table, I could appreciate the movement and firmness of Ulga's hands, I began to drift into a tranquil state.

I could hear in the far distance someone calling my name. It was Ulga. "Ms. Allis" she said softly, you are finished. I didn't know what she had done, but it certainly did relax me. "Oh "I responded, "Finished already?" She smiled and pointed to the clock, "I can give you more time if you like. My next customer canceled". "I wish that I had more time, but I am on a schedule today" I replied as I made my way off of the table. Plus, I knew more time meant more money. I went to the dressing room to put my clothes back on. I felt so much better. I combed my hair, thanked Ulga again and made my way downstairs to the nail area. Jean, the manicurist was waiting for me. She suggested that I get my pedicure first. The water was warm and sudsy. She turned on the vibrator to massage my feet and lightly brushed over them with a loafer sponge. I enjoyed coming here because they did such a great job. After the pedicure, Jean gave me a few minutes and then moved me to the manicure section. I selected a bright color to make me feel pretty. She gave me a complete manicure with a hand massage. As Jean applied the polish to both my toenails and fingernails, I looked out of the big plate glass window in the front of the salon, and felt the warmth of the sun shining through. I knew that I wasn't going to risk smudging my polish trying to reach into my purse to find money, so they were content to let me sit and wait for my nails to dry. After a reasonable amount of time, I reached into my purse to get the money to pay. As I left the salon I felt rejuvenated and ready to really deal with the issue at hand… the man that called himself my father.

Chapter Nine

I reached for my phone to make a phone call and remembered that Lynn had called me. I thought that I would give her a call back. Lynn was always good for some interesting conversation. I dialed her number and she picked up on the third ring. "Hey girl, where have you been? You know that I have been trying to reach you. Is everything alright?" Lynn was a fast talker. "Yeah, I am fine "I said sensing that she wanted to tell me something more. "I was talking to Sister Ida Mae on the other Sunday. She mentioned that her new neighbor Kevin, his father would be in town for the next few months. Lynn had been interrogating Sis. Ida Mae about him, I'm sure. Lynn was a bit of a flirt and self-appointed F.B.I. agent. So, I said to her "What… you going after senior citizens now?" We both chuckled and she said "It's getting so now girl, that all a man have to be is breathing!" We laughed harder. "I haven't seen him, but I am sure that Ms. Ida Mae probably could describe him to a tee. We are having Family and Friends Day at church and she probably will not miss the opportunity to invite them". "By the way", she paused and suddenly asked me, "If you aren't busy at your church why don't you come on over and visit with us. If Kevin and his father do show up, it will give you a chance to see them both." I didn't answer her right away. Lynn asked again and said "Oh come on, you know that you would like to see him again". I was smiling at the thought of another meeting with him, so I said that I would give it some thought. Then Lynn said as though a light bulb had come on, "If they are still in town I will invite them to my party! I could always use some more handsome males on the guest list". I kept smiling as I went out the door.

Lynn was right. I wouldn't mind seeing Kevin again. Something about him reminded me of myself. He was a handsome guy with what seemed like a wonderful sense of humor. I thought of him as someone who I could probably just hang out with. I was comfortable around him, although for some reason, I thought that he was younger than me. These days' guys come with a lot of baggage. Half of them have little or no education, which means that they probably don't have a job or they are living at home with their parents (mostly their mamas). The other half has some baby mama drama going on. They can't hook a verb up with a noun or they are taking or selling pharmaceuticals. I don't need that kind of chaos in my life. For the short time that I spent with Kevin, he impressed me to be the kind of guy that was on the right track with his life. I've met a lot of guys in a lot of places, but very few in churches. I took that as a possible good sign.

Now I was hungry and wanted to get something to eat. My mind said that a nice fresh salad would be good, but my stomach was thinking about something that would provide a little more calorie intake. I begin to go down the list of fast food places that I would pass on my way home.

Chapter Ten

I stopped at Subway and got a sandwich. I let them turn it into a salad on bread by putting tomatoes, lettuce, mushrooms and everything else that I could get on it. I had all of my nutrients right in front of me. I turned to the refrigerator to get something to drink. I fought off the urge to get a soda and settled for a bottle of water. I felt a little tired, but my thoughts were still very much active. Could this day have changed the rest of my life? Had I really talked to the man that could be my natural father? I wanted to take some time and re-run our conversation through my mind, slowly.

I have always wanted to know who my father was although I wasn't suffering psychologically from not knowing. As a young girl, I always had a vision of what I thought he would look like in my own mind before my mother described him to me. I thought that he would be a dark complexion man with coarse hair, like me. I figured that he would stand about six feet tall with a medium build, not like me. I had my mothers' height and build. He probably was a decent dresser with nice teeth, a coy smile and piercing eyes. Now, it was a possibility that I would get a chance to meet him. That thought was a little unsettling, scary even.

I remember what my mother told me about my father when the conversation came up. She had no pictures of him, so she described him to me in her own words as a dark chocolate complexion man, medium height with a firmly built body frame. His eyes were medium light brown, he had full lips and a small well shaped nosed. His hair was thick and kinky. He wore a beard and mustache which he kept neatly cut and trimmed. He had a tattoo of a small bulldog on the inside of his left upper arm. Mama said that he had a great sense of humor and a million dollar smile. Putting the two descriptions together, I could envision a handsome guy as my father.

I knew that I wanted to meet the man behind the phone call. I wanted to be prepared for whatever. I needed to be prayed up and strong enough to deal with the planned encounter. After all, it is not every day that a forty-year old woman gets to meet her father whom she had never seen for the first time! I heard the man "Herman" which is my father's name; say that he had been looking for me also. I wondered how long he had been looking. I grew up with a step-father. I don't recall anyone saying that I would get to spend any time with my natural father. You know how some children get to spend weekends or holidays with the other parent, that didn't happen to me. I always questioned why. I wondered if I was anything like him. Did I look like him, act like him, if we had anything in common. I felt like pieces of me were missing. I wasn't sure about why I acted or felt certain ways about things. Most people said that I was like my mother. This may have been true, but on the inside I knew that all of me was not like her. It was those other attributes that were not like her that made me question if I had any of my father's characteristics living in me. In my mind, I had my own personal images and opinions about the man that was my father.

I thought that I had grown out of the need to have a daddy. My stepfather filled that role really well. Although he wasn't perfect and tended to drink a little too much at times, he loved me, and I loved him as the only father that I knew. Strangely enough, when my stepfather died, my desire to find my natural father emerged again. Every child needs their father in their life. It is wonderful if it can be their natural father. Girls tend to look for men and husbands that are like their fathers. In some cases, I don't know if that is a good thing or not. I thank God that my stepfather was a good man, a good provider. That made it easier not to miss my natural father as much. However the question still remained, "Who was my father"?

I felt sleep coming on, so I finished my meal and cleaned up the kitchen. I made my way to the bedroom. It had been a rather long day.

After a quick shower, I turned on the television and got into the bed. My sheets were crisp and smelled so good, like a field of flowers. I laid right in the middle of the bed, trying to clear my mind and relax. I don't even remember when I drifted off to sleep.

Chapter Eleven

Much to my surprise I rested very well. The sun was peeping through the blinds as I turned toward the windows. I laid in the bed waiting for my thoughts to fill up my brain. I had so much to do, yet I just couldn't focus. I was glad that I didn't have to go to work, it was the weekend. I had been so busy with my own life that I couldn't really get excited about Lynn's party which was tonight.

I laid there putting together what I was going to wear in my mind. I wanted to match her color scheme. I wanted to be comfortable too. I liked the freedom of movement when I was coordinating an affair, so my outfit had to be right. I thought that maybe I would wear a dress or a long skirt. That decision would depend on the weather. Just to be safe, maybe I needed to consider a pants suit also. I was sure that Lynn had spent a good amount of her time looking for the right outfit. Lynn loved shopping. Her entire outfit would be color coordinated. I am sure that her hair would be done with every strand in place. Her nails and toes would coordinate with her outfit. She would want every eye on her, complimenting her appearance. She delighted in attention, although she would not say so. Tonight, the spotlight should be on her, it was her night.

As I rolled to the side of the bed, waiting for the blood to start circulating in my legs, I prayed. I still hadn't wrapped my mind around all of the happenings of the past few days, but I was trusting that the Lord would make it clear to me. I sat there for a few moments hoping that I would get an instant sign or something, but I didn't, so I made my way into the bathroom. My own personal thoughts began to fill my head slowly. The warm water from the shower started to make my body come alive. It was going to be a full day. So I knew that I needed to have an organized plan and a clear thought process in order to make it through the day not frazzled.

"Ahh" I felt better. I started moving with intent. I had some errands that required me to physically handle before tonight. Thankfully the few things that I needed to do only required a phone call to activate. I started with a call to Ms. Wynfield at the Fields of Pleasure Hall, that's where Lynn's Affair was going to be held. I wanted to confirm everything one last time. "Hello, The Fields of Pleasure Ballroom, Ms. Wynfield speaking, how may I assist you today?" I was surprised that she answered the phone. "Hello Ms. Wynfied, this is Ms. Allis calling. "Oh, Good Morning Ms. Allis" she said "How are you doing today?" "I am doing well" was my reply. Then the particulars of our conversation started. I felt really good about choosing Ms. Wynfield to coordinate the arrangements for the hall. She assured me that things would go as we discussed. She was so professional. I enjoyed doing business with her.

I called the photographer and the limousine company to confirm the information on their contract one last time. I didn't want anyone getting amnesia at the last minute. Lynn was going to be surprised because her daughter arranged to have a limousine pick her up from her house. Lynn probably would have put that money towards some more chicken or something. Lynn was hilarious. I certainly hope that no one pissed her off today before she got to the party, because she also could be a whip! I thought to call her but I didn't want to be bombarded with one hundred and one questions. So unless she called me I would just see her tonight when she arrived.

I finished making my calls and now I could go out and run my errands. I wanted to have my nails done and pick up a bouquet of live flowers for Lynn's table. The hall provided artificial centerpieces for the other tables. I just thought it would be nice for her to have some live flowers and she could take them home after the party.

I went downstairs, opened up the blinds in the living room and peeped out. The sun was bright, the sky was clear. The sun's warmth felt good upon my face. As I stood there I began to thank God for his goodness towards me. For the most part, I have had a good life. Even as I stood there and thought about my "father" issues, I concluded that I was still blessed.

I moved to the kitchen but that thought followed me. I knew that some people never got beyond the fact that one of their natural parents didn't raise them. Some of them never knew who their natural parents were. Some of them were given to another family member to be raised. They carried that baggage with them for years. Although that was part of my story, I thank God that I was not consumed with that aspect of my life from day to day. I wondered, could it be because the Lord was always working it out in my spirit as I grew up. All that I needed, the Lord provided for me. He guided every facet of my life because he knew this would be in my life. He sheltered and strengthened me at the same time. He gave me a voice, a bold voice to speak up for myself. He put in me hidden self-esteem because he knew that others would try to treat me as the black sheep. He opened doors, cleared paths, created opportunities just so that I would not sink into the sea of misery that others seemed to have done because of a situation like mine. Praise the Lord! I had a great mom that directed me to my father, my heavenly father. He does what my natural father should have done.

I heard someone knocking at the door. That caused my heart to skip a beat. Now who in the world could that be I was thinking as I went to look out of the peephole. It was my mailman Jay, standing there with an envelope in his hand. I opened the door. "Hey Ms. Allis", he said. "Hi Jay, how are you doing?" I replied. "I have a registered letter for you. Sign here for me please". I hesitated to take the letter at first; my mind went back to that bright colored envelope that came in the mail awhile back. I signed for the letter, Jay said goodbye and I closed the door. Umm, let me see who this is from. I looked at the return address, no name but it had a post office box number on it and a city zip code. My antennas went up and my curiosity peaked. I thought to myself, I'm not opening any mystery mail. I went over to the window and held it up to the light to see if my x-ray vision would allow me to see something on the inside. Nothing. I shook it and smelled it to see if I could get a clue. Nothing. So then I decided just to open it up. I carefully tore open the end and let the paper inside slide out onto the table. I picked it up, unfolded the outer sheet and discovered that inside was a picture of a handsome older man. Who could this be?

Chapter Twelve

The phone rang and I ignored it. My attention was focused on the picture that I held tightly in my hand. I starred at the picture, reviewing every feature of the man's face. It seemed to be a photo from back in the day, around the forties or fifties era. His skin was a dark chocolate. His hair was neatly cut and shaped, so was his mustache. His eyes were bright and clear with heavy eyebrows over them. His facial shape was somewhat oblong, yet full. His smile was wide just giving a peek at his bright teeth. My grandmother would say that he was easy on the eyes.

I turned the picture over and on the back was a sticker with a typed written name -Herman Louis Allis. I couldn't blink. I had to catch my breath. All of a sudden my mind went blank. I looked up towards the window and then back down at the picture. I re-examined the face closer. My spirit was quiet but my voice whispered out loud, "This must be my father".

The phone was ringing again, but I was in the twilight zone. Cautiously I made my way to it. I pushed the button and said "Hello". It was Lynn's daughter on the other end. I must have sounded like I wasn't really there. She said slowly, "H-e-l-l-o, Ms. Allis" like she wasn't sure that she had dialed the right number. I pulled myself together and said "Hey baby, how are things going?" She said "Okay, are you alright?" "Oh yeah, I'm fine" trying to disguise that my mind was really somewhere else. We chatted for a few minutes about her mother's excitement. She told me that Lynn had gone all out on her outfit. We laughed and talked about the entertainment for tonight and then she hung up. My attention immediately turned back to the picture. I didn't have time to investigate it further because I had a nail appointment. I slipped it into my purse. I reached for the polish that I wanted the nail technician to use and put it in there too. I had brought some nail polish that matched the color of my lipstick. Lynn wasn't going to be the only one that would be coordinated I thought to myself.

As I was driving to the nail salon I knew that I needed to pace myself. This was going to be a long day. I thought about the card, the phone messages, the conversation and now the picture. Could they all be connected somehow?

Chapter Thirteen

I had completed all of my errands and was on the way back home when I thought about getting some gas in my car. I didn't like for my gas needle to be under a quarter of a tank. So I stopped at the gas station to take care of that. I thought to myself, as I reached for my money, what happened to the days when they use to have a gas attendant that would pump your gas and wash your windshields. Things are so different now. Women need to know how to do it all nowadays. We are the ones that own most of the cars anyway. My father was a Master Mechanic. He taught me how to change a flat tire, check my oil and pump my gas. Looking back it was a good thing that I learned it. I found my money and balled it up in my hand before I went inside to pay for my gas. I never took my purse inside with me. The guy behind the glass asked me what pump I was using, I told him pump number two. He acted like he didn't understand my language and started pointing to the pumps outside. I held up two fingers while I looked him dead in the eyes. Then he shook his head and said "Yeah yeah". I said to myself as I walked away, learn the language if you are going to do the business.

I finished pumping my gas, unlocked my car, got in started it up and watched the needle move to full. I buckled up, turned out of the parking lot and headed towards home.

Chapter Fourteen

I was getting excited. In a few hours I would be in the midst of Lynn's party and prayerfully having a good time. All the planning had been done and if all went well it should be a wonderful evening. Lynn was a good friend. I didn't know all of the people that she had invited but I am sure that they were good people too. She loved to laugh, eat and dance. We had planned to have a lot of Old School music playing throughout the evening.

I knew in my mind what I was going to wear. I wanted to be comfortable. I liked my clothes to express me. I was no size ten, but I think that even at my size my clothes could look good and fit. I didn't want to spend the night pulling at, tucking in or adjusting nothing that I had on.

I came in the house and put down my purse. I checked the phone for messages, there weren't any. I was surprised that Lynn hadn't called me. She probably was far too busy getting herself into Diva mode. I headed for my bedroom. I begin to lay my outfit out on the bed. It was too quiet in the house, so I turned to the radio to find a station for some pre- partying music to get myself in the mood.

The music helped. Before I knew it I was singing and stepping around the bedroom. After I laid everything out, I decided to take a relaxing bath. I reached for the Dial soap but laughed at myself when I put it back in the soap dish. I thought to myself, tonight I am going to use the good stuff. So, I reached for my Bath and Body Works collection. I relaxed in the tub as the music played in the background. Yeah, this was going to be a great night I thought as I reclined in the tub. When I finished soaking, I felt really good. The water started to cool so I pulled myself up out of the tub to dry off. I checked the clock to make sure that I was in my time frame. I didn't want to be late. My plan was to get there and make sure that things were set up right. Although, I felt like Ms. Wynfield would be on the case.

I styled my hair three different ways before I decided on the style that I would wear. I put my clothes on and everything fell right into place. I felt good! When I checked myself out in my full length mirror everything was perfect. My bra was supporting the girls, so they wouldn't be hanging out on their own. The panty girdle was holding without making me feel like a sausage and my dress was sexy without being sluttish. I was comfortable and modestly in vogue. I put on my makeup and accessories. I did a final check like the "Fonz" did on Happy Days and approved my look.

I gathered up everything that I needed my keys, purse and the program folder. I turned on the night light over the stove so that the house would not be dark when I returned home. I grabbed my shawl and headed for the door.

Chapter Fifteen

I arrived at the hall around six o'clock. There were a few cars on the parking lot so I was able to park close. I grabbed my shopping bag that had some personal items in it from the back seat and started across the lot. I could hear the music as I approached the building. That meant that the DJ had arrived.

I felt good. As I entered the building Ms. Wynfield met me at the door. She welcomed me with a smile and said that she was glad that I had arrived early. She wanted to show me around in case there was something that needed to be adjusted. She took my things and put them in her office. I liked her. She was so organized. When I stepped into the ballroom I was thrilled. Ms. Wynfield had nailed it! The color scheme, the placement of the tables and chairs, the food buffet, everything was on point. The centerpieces were gorgeous and the head table was beautifully decorated. As I continued to walk through the room I noticed the backdrop for taking personal pictures for the photographer and even the scent of the air was inviting. I know that I am a hard person to please when it comes to event planning, but this exceeded my expectations. I turned to Ms. Wynfield and gave her an emotional, yes!, with my thumbs up in the air gesture. She smiled and we hugged as a way of touching and agreeing.

All I had to do now was wait for the guest of honor and the guest to arrive. Since I had a few moments, I asked Ms. Wynfield if she had a quiet place that I could sit and review the program that I had put together. She directed me to her office. I really just needed a space to compose myself and talk to the Lord. I always asked the Lord to bless the work of my heart and hands.

Lynn didn't want a lot of pomp and circumstance. She wanted the evening to be filled with music, dancing, laughter, food and friends. So I had developed a program that would capture that. Lynn would make her grand entrance with an introduction that I wrote for her. Then a few people, at designated times, would take her down memory lane with their remarks about her. Her children wanted to present her with something special and then Lynn would give comments at the end. The rest of the evening would be spent doing what she had requested, dancing, eating and socializing.

People were beginning to arrive. I checked my watch. It was six-thirty. Lynn was supposed to arrive at seven-fifteen. As more guest showed up, they were welcomed by the assigned hostesses. I could see some of the expressions on their faces as they entered the ballroom. Ms. Wynfield had adjusted the lightening to make the room more atmospheric. Everyone looked so nice. I knew some of the guest so we exchanged comments and had small conversations while I waited for the limousine. I paced the floor. The limousine driver said that he would call me on my cell phone when he was ten minutes away. That would give me time to make the announcement and settle people down. I knew that everyone wasn't going to be there, but quite a few people were.

I was trying to keep my cool when I looked up and saw a very handsome face. It was Kevin! Wow! I was speechless and nervous. As our eyes met, I smiled and started towards him. He was smiling. It wasn't a nervous kind of feeling you get when you are intimately attracted to someone. It was more of an, it is really good to see you, I was wondering how you were doing kind of feeling. When I drew close to him I blurted out, "Hey Kevin" as though we were old friends. He said "Hello Sandy". I was shocked that he remembered my name. You know how guys can be. If it ain't nothing in it for them they quickly put your name on the do not call list, like you got the plague or something. "It is good to see you again", he said. "Likewise" I said with a broad grin. "I know right," he chuckled "especially in this setting with adults and no children crawling over our feet". We both laughed out loud remembering our at church experience. "Oh, Sandy forgive my manners; let me introduce my date, my Dad".

When we turned, his date, his Dad, had left us standing there. We laughed again. Just then the phone rang. It was the limousine driver. I apologized to Kevin and told him that I needed to take the call. He said, "Sure, no problem. Hopefully we will get a chance to talk later". I confirmed by nodding my head.

Chapter Sixteen

After taking the call from the limousine driver, I returned to the room to inform the guest that Lynn would be arriving in about seven minutes. I briefly gave them some additional information. The programs were on the tables like menus. The DJ already knew what song to play softly for her entrance. His cue would be when she stepped into the doorway with her son and I began to read her introduction. Everyone seemed relaxed and excited at the same time. I left the room and stood at the front door with her son. Within a few minutes the limousine pulled up. When Lynn stepped out of the limousine, she looked amazing! Our eyes met and she reached out for a hug. I told her immediately as we embraced, "You pulled out all of the stops on this outfit." She grinned and said "Oh girl, this old thing" we both laughed uncontrollably. I loved Lynn spirit.

She wore a peach colored, tailored made polished satin bodice blouse with sheer sleeves that had satin fabric French cuffs and collar. The blouse neatly tucked into her polished satin pants that had a shimmering sheer peach over layered skirt that opened in the front. It flowed as she walked. Her son leaned over to give her a kiss and whispered "Mom you look beautiful". She said "Now don't make me mess up this make-up job that I paid far too much for by crying". She started fanning her face with her hands to hold back the tears. She took a deep breath and said" Okay let the party begin!"

I told Lynn how her entrance would be done so that she wouldn't give her son the blues. He already knew what the plan was. I told Lynn to just follow his lead. She agreed. I left them in the hall and moved to the podium. The DJ closed out the music that was playing and started the music for Lynn's entrance. All eyes turned towards the doorway. When Lynn and her son stepped into view, a hush fell over the room. Lynn was breathtaking. As the music played, I began to read the introduction. Lynn's son escorted her into the room and seated her at the head table. It was perfectly timed. Before Lynn sat down we immediately played Stevie Wonder's rendition of the Happy Birthday song. Ms. Wynfield who was right on time, turned the house lights up a little more at the end of the song. Lynn's cousin, who was a minister, came forward to bless the food. Lynn then took her seat. The DJ started playing Jazz music and the hostesses started directing tables to the buffet.

People were mingling and coming to the head table to chat with Lynn. Her daughter and her son were seated at the head table with her also. It was a party atmosphere. Lynn was beaming. I watched from afar to make sure that things were going as planned. The DJ was doing a great job with the music. Lynn wanted Old School music and he was cranking it out. The Temptations, Stylistics, Marvin Gaye and the Whispers were all in the room. After she finished playing in her plate pretending to eat, she hit the dance floor. She was in her zone, laughing, talking, smiling and being surrounded by those she loved and loved her back.

I took this time to make my way over to the buffet line to get something to eat. The food looked good and the setup was nice. After going down the line, I looked around the room for someplace to sit. There was a table not too far from the head table so I headed for it. As I got to the chair, it was unexpectedly pulled out by Kevin. "Oh thank you very much" I smiled in appreciation. "No problem, you look like you have your hands full" he replied. Kevin was a gentleman and very charismatic. He had a beautiful smile and an inviting tone to his voice. He was dressed appropriately for the occasion, not like a yo boy. He took my plate and sat down beside me. We started to talk. Although the music was pumping in the background I was in tuned to his every word. We started out with small talk, the place, the food the people. Then he asked about me and Lynn's friendship. We talked like old friends that were catching up. Then I said to him "Where is your Dad?" He turned to scan the room and said "That is a good question.

I have enjoyed sitting here talking to you so much, I forgot that he had come with me". Maybe you better go and find him", I whispered," I would love to meet him". "My Dad fits in wherever he goes. He doesn't need a babysitter. He is Mr. Personality. He is probably sitting at some table captivating someone with one of his funny stories. However, I will go and find him and bring him back to meet you". "Okay, I will be sitting right here", I said.

I looked up to see that Lynn had taken off her shoes. She was twirling and throwing her hips around to the music. Her hands were up in the air and her diva girl hairstyle was on its way to becoming a pony tail. The noise level had gone up a few octaves, but it was okay the party was jumping. It was rewarding just to see that Lynn was having a good time. All of the planning was paying off. I turned my attention to my food as I also watched everyone enjoy themselves. The Hot Wings were delicious. I was careful not to drip any of the Blue Cheese dip on my clothes. The salad was fresh and crisp, umm good! I was putting my face in my plate when I looked up and saw Kevin making his way back to the table. I quickly wiped around my mouth and dabbed my face to remove any excess perspiration. I was thinking to myself as he approached how well-mannered he seemed. I didn't want him to think that I was a little pig. I poised myself as he reached the table and sat down. "I told my dad where I was, so he should be along shortly". "Okay, is he having a good time?" I asked. "Yes. My dad could be the life of the party at a funeral." We laughed and continued our conversation while I tried not to devour my food in front of him.

Chapter Seventeen

Kevin liked to travel. So taking a job with the government that allowed him that opportunity was a joy for him. He said that he grew up moving from one place to another so it was kind of in his blood. His dad was a military man and his mother died when he was two years old. His dad raised him with the help of some other family members. It was obvious that he loved his dad. Kevin was six years younger than I, but his conversation was very mature. He worked for the Department of Treasury and his dad was a retired Army Officer that had also worked as a civilian for the FBI. His facial expression was endearing when he spoke of how grateful he was that his dad was still in his life.

The lights were turned up and Lynn's son and daughter were at the microphone. This was the point in the party when they were going to allow some of Lynn's family and friends to talk about their relationship with her. They didn't want to keep stopping the party's flow, so they decided to allow the three assigned people that were going to speak, to do it one behind another. This would give Lynn some time to sit down and breathe. They made some funny comments and laughter filled the room as they told their stories. At the end of their speaking, her children presented Lynn with a gift from the both of them. It was a lovely diamond necklace. I could see the sparkle from across the room. Lynn was so surprised; she started wiping her cheeks as the tears fell from her eyes. She gave them both a hug and kiss. As others came to her to get a closer look, she ran her fingers over it and pressed it close to her chest. "Wow, someone has some money" Kevin whispered softly. I smiled and said "You don't know her story. She deserves it". Kevin smiled as the lights were turned back down and the party resumed. "Yeah, we all have a story don't we? I have been talking so much I haven't given you a chance to share. So tell me Sandy what is your story?"

Just then Kevin's dad came to the table. He was polite but seemed distracted as he interrupted our conversation. He stood bent over beside Kevin's chair with his head towards the floor "Well Kevin" he said "I found you, and from what I have heard you are sitting with the second most important lady in the room. I was still eating and chewing my food. When I realized that he was referring to me, I wiped my mouth to turn and look at him. "Hello. I'm Kevin's dad, and I've been told that you are the lovely lady responsible for putting this evening together. His head was still bent over and reaching for my hand. I stretched out my hand to greet him. His touch was reserved but our eyes locked for a moment as though we were familiar with each other but wasn't sure how. From what I could see in the dimly lit room, his smile was wide and bright like Kevin's. He kissed the back of my hand and then quickly turned towards Kevin to excuse himself. He told him that he had left a young lady at another table and wanted to get back to her before she got restless. "Yeah Pop, just remember who you came with" Kevin said in a jokingly way. He left the table and made his way back across the room through the crowd of people that were dancing on the floor. 'I have to keep my eyes on him. Tomorrow he will be complaining about his arthritis", Kevin said humorously.

Kevin asked me if I wanted to dance. I begged off. So then he asked me if we could maybe go into the lobby area where it was a little less noise and movement. I wanted to finish eating my good food, but the lady in me agreed. My ears needed a break anyway. He asked "Do you want some punch?" "Yes, that would be nice" I said. We made our way out to the lobby and found two comfortable chairs. I could still see just about everything that was going on in the main room in case I needed to address something.

"Whew" I exhaled as I sunk into the cushioned chair. "Are you tired?" Kevin inquired. "Kinda yeah, kinda no" I said "but it feels good to be on the other side of the planning aspects of this affair. "From what I can see you really did a great job. Is this something that you do all of the time?"

"No, I'm a school teacher looking for a real paying job." I was being sarcastic. We laughed. "I like to organize and see the outcome of things. So I took up the challenge of being an events coordinator part-time. I really like it, but it can be all consuming at times "I replied. "Why?" he looked concerned. "Because I have a little perfectionist living on the inside of me that can sometimes make my planning experiences stressful." "Did you always want to be a teacher?" he asked. "No" I quietly said, "I wanted to be a psychologist, you know, try and figure out people's behavior. But my life went in another direction. I'm not upset about it because God has really blessed my life. He has ordered my steps and directed my path. So now here I am trying to figure out my own past and behavior. I have some personal issues that I am dealing with from my childhood. I guess I am more curious then troubled by them." We sat and exchanged more conversation, laughed and enjoyed each other's company as the moments slipped by. Kevin seemed so attentive to my conversation. I had to catch myself. I was feeling far too relaxed with telling this man my life's story. I paused and then said very slowly "Soooo ....Kevin maybe we need to get back and mingle with the other folks." He hesitated and made a side grin facial expression, but then said "Alright, can I give you my contact information; I would love to just sit and talk with you some more, let me find a pen and a piece of paper. I hope that I'm not being too forward or fresh, but I haven't met a lot of people on casual basis since I've been here. My dad is visiting, but soon he will be going back home. It just seems like I've known you for years. I hope that doesn't make you feel uncomfortable". "Oh no" I said. He patted his jacket for a pen and looked around for a piece of paper. I could tell that he didn't want to leave that spot. I reached into my purse "Let me help you out. Here's my telephone number". I wrote my first name and number on a church envelope. If you want to get together for coffee or something, give me a call. I would love to hear more of your story." I looked at him and strangely enough I felt at ease with sharing my phone number with him. He didn't strike me as a guy who had some maniac at home that would find my number and make me sorry that I gave it to him by calling me with her jealousy issues.

Chapter Eighteen

The DJ had shifted the music to slow jams. It was getting a little late, but the party was still going strong. There were still some party animals left, even though some people were beginning to leave. Lynn was still being the social butterfly. There was still food left on the buffet so I went to get some dessert. It had been a wonderful evening. I certainly hoped that Lynn felt the same way. I found a spot to sit down to enjoy my dessert. As I looked around the room I could tell that the baby boomers were diehards. Everyone seemed friendly and I am sure that everyone had a story. I sat a little longer and my bladder started calling. I looked towards the lobby where the restrooms were, and thought that I better start making my way to the ladies room. I spoke to a few people as I headed towards that direction.

Much to my surprise there were only a few ladies inside the restroom. Some were retouching their makeup and adjusting their clothing. I headed for an unoccupied stall. Even in the restroom the party atmosphere was going strong. Someone started singing a song that could be heard from the main room. After I made my contribution to the sewer system and made it disappear, I moved toward the sink. A lady was pulling up her knee-high stockings. She said, "Girls, I have almost danced right out of my stockings!" We all laughed. I took it that she was having a good time. I finished washing my hands and checking my appearance. Then I opened the door. As I turned to the right, I saw Kevin leaving out of the door with his father beside him. I was too much of a lady to holler out after him. I was okay; I remembered that I had his contact information. I made my way back into the party and Lynn caught my eye. She was waving her hand for me to come in her direction. When I reached her, she hugged me with one of those rock you from side to side, gasping for breath hugs. She was bursting with excitement. "Ally (that's what she called me), this was the best party that I have ever had! Thank you, thank you, thank you! I may have to pay you a little more! "Yeah right " I said through my unbelieving smile. It was good to see her so excited and pleased. This is why I enjoyed doing these events. It gave me inner pleasure to see the excitement and joy that it brought to others. Lynn was a good friend and I wanted it to be really nice for her. "You know that we have to get together and recap. It was so much that happened tonight; I just have to have time to take it all in" she blurted out over the music. "No problem", I said, "now go and enjoy your final minutes because we are getting ready to bring this to an end, girlfriend." She twisted herself off into the crowd as the DJ announced last dance. It was a line dance of course.

Everyone that was still there made their way to the floor. The DJ did some thank you's through the music while people were on the dance floor. When the music stopped and the house lights went up some people looked drained. That was a good look in that it meant that they had partied hard. As people were leaving I felt a sense of accomplishment. The many months of planning had paid off. Lynn and I walked out together, chatting and laughing. Her son put her in the car and then walked me to mine. He thanked me again and said good night.

I sat there in silence for a moment thanking God for the ability that he had given me to be creative and to coordinate different types of affairs. It's not always easy, but somehow he always brings me through. Lynn blew the horn to make sure that I was okay. I started my car up and started to move from the parking space. I turned on my radio to listen to some soft music for my ride home.

I replayed the events of the night in my mind, especially the moments that I spent with Kevin. He was such a gentleman. I sincerely enjoyed talking to him in a good friend kind of way. Now that I had his contact information, I surely would try and connect with him. Maybe I would get a chance to meet his Dad in a more structured atmosphere. It was something about his dad that I couldn't put my fingers on, something that seemed familiar. Oh well, I wasn't going to worry about it tonight I was too tired. I'd better focus on getting home safely.

Chapter Nineteen

The morning sun hit my face and I recalled getting home last night. I remembered taking a quickie wash down and crawling into my bed; half washed and falling right to sleep. That's one good thing about being single and living alone; you didn't have to go to bed smelling all fresh and stuff if you didn't want to. I remembered that the light on my answering machine was blinking when I came in, but I was too tired to even see who it was that had called.

I laid in bed and stretched for a while. I had nothing pressing to do today and that's how I had planned it. I found myself talking to the Lord and thanking him for his goodness. I felt better after prayer. As I rolled to the side of the bed, the blinking light on the phone caught my attention. It could wait a little longer. I got up and took a nice long shower. Since I had nothing to do today I put on my robe and went downstairs to have a leisurely breakfast. It was nice not to be hurried. I opened up the blinds to a bright sunny day. Again the blinking light on the phone caught my eyes. I put water in the teapot to make a cup of hot tea. I pushed the button on the answering machine to listen to the message while I reached for the cream in the refrigerator. "Hey, Sandy" the message began "I just wanted to check and see if you made it home okay. I wasn't sure if this was your home, cell or a business number, but when you get this message I trust that you are okay. I enjoyed the party and the evening. I hope to talk to you soon, Kevin". I almost dropped the cream right in the middle of the floor! How special was that? I thought. After a few moments of pause, I gave it some real thought. I am usually a good judge of character. He didn't strike me to be a stalker or someone that I would regret that I had given my number to. This was probably a genuine call of concern. That is what a gentleman would do, I thought to myself. The teapot started to whistle so I removed it from the stove. I poured the hot water over my tea bag and pressed play again to listen to the message one more time.

Sipping on tea and hearing Kevin's message were the makings for the beginning of a good day. I lounged around looking at TV, reading and listening to music. My mind kept going back to Kevin's phone message. Maybe I should just call Kevin and let him know that I did get his message and to thank him. This would let him know that he did have a contact number for me, be it business or private. I also wanted him to know that I appreciated his concern. After chewing on that thought like a dog with a bone, I decided to call him back and let him know that I did make it home alright. It was the polite thing to do. Then I would see where the conversation would go from there. I checked the caller ID to see if his name showed up. It didn't, just his number.

As I reached for the phone it rang. On the third ring I answered. "Hello" I said softly. "Hello, Sandy". I recognized the voice immediately. My heart started to beat vigorously. I said "yes", trying not to let the excitement that I felt come across in my voice. "This is Kevin." "Kevin, how nice to hear from you" I said. I could have got an academy award for playing this part like Bette Davis. She was noted for keeping her cool under pressure. "I tried to reach you last night just to see if you had arrived home safely". "Thank you!" I replied light heartedly. I saw the light blinking on my phone when I got in, but I was so tired I went straight to bed. I didn't want to run the risk of someone having some drama that I would have to deal with and ruin a wonderful evening". We both chuckled. "Well, I am glad to see that I did have the right contact number for you". "I was going to return your call. I probably should have done it sooner, but I slept in late" I said in an apologetic way. "It was very considerate of you to do that". I tried not to sound like I was rambling. After a moment of silence, Kevin said, "Okay, I hope that you have a great day. Now that I have your number, you don't mind if I keep in touch do you?" "I would like that" I said holding back my excitement. "Maybe we could follow up with that coffee or lunch date?" I blurted out. OOH, I thought to myself.

I hope that wasn't to forward or sounded too desperate. Too bad, it was out there now. I liked Kevin's company and I didn't see anything wrong with him knowing it. "Sure that's a plan" he responded quickly. "Take care of yourself; I hope to talk with you again soon". "Okay, take care, goodbye" I replied. "Goodbye" he said and hung up.

I put the portable phone back on the hook. I rested my hand on the receiver while I scribbled his number from the caller ID on the pad. I probably was one of the few people in the world that still had a landline phone. It was a nice conversation. There were still some things about Kevin that I found interesting. At Lynn's party we didn't have time to go into depth about his dad and his career. I definitely felt a connection between us. Prayerfully we will get a chance to explore and share our stories further.

Chapter Twenty

Today was Sunday. I rested all day yesterday. I looked forward to going to church and being in worship. It took a lot for me to miss church. Sometimes, I would laugh about attending White Sheet Baptist with my friends where Rev. Serta was the very fine Pastor. I know that sometimes the body needs rest or circumstances may prevent you from getting there. However, I felt that if you were saved, you really should want to be in worship services (Hebrews 10:25). It is a source of strength and encouragement.

As I stood in front of my closet, I tried to decide on which outfit to wear. I was blessed. Clothing was not an issue for me. I could dress it up with all the frills or dress down. I thought to myself, I should have laid my outfit out last night. It didn't matter; it was going to be simple today. I didn't feel like over accentuating. Some of the sisters did a real good job with matching the hats, jewelry, accessories and shoes. I never wanted to make me the center of attention. Sometimes, you can block the view of Jesus by what you wear. Today, that was not going to be happening with me. I reached into my closet and pulled out a Navy Blue Travelers suit. I loved the material these garments were made of. They had no wrinkles and fit me so comfortably. I had plenty of scarves, so I found one that would match perfectly. I could simply wrap it around my neck. My shoes were Navy Blue and flat. I was ready.

Service was very uplifting. The choir was on point with the music and the sermon was delivered plainly and spiritedly. You could hear the hallelujahs and amens' all over the church. The Word of God had a way of bringing forth different responses from the congregation. The Lord was worthy of all praise!

After church, I spent some time speaking to a few people. With my peripheral view, I could see Sis. Alberta. She was making her way to me. She always had a complaint ending with, I'm just saying, Praise the Lord! Not realizing that she had said too much when she said it. I braced myself for the one-sided, um-hum conversation that was about to take place. For some reason, she felt that the ministry that I served on was her personal sounding board for when she had a complaint. This was not the Sunday and I was not the one! As she pressed her way through the other members that were standing around in the aisle, Marva caught my eye. She probably read the expression on my face and she started toward me also. I was glad that my friends knew me well enough to interpret my body language. Sis Alberta and Marva e both reached me at the same time, but of course Sis. Alberta was going to get her say out first. I allowed her to start and after a few um hum's, I interrupted her by saying "Sis Alberta, help me serve you better by putting your concern in writing and giving it back to me. That would really help me, okay". She didn't expect that, but she conceded to doing so because Marva was standing there. As she walked away, I thanked God for his grace. Marva smiled and patted me on the shoulder. She asked me if I was alright. I said "Yeah girl, I am fine." "Okay, then let's go have some lunch. Let me see if Dessa wants to go also". We had some small talk and decided where we were going to eat.

When I got to my car I thought that today might be a good day to tell Marva and Dessa about what I had been doing for the past few months in relation to my father. I hadn't shared with them about the search or the progress. It wasn't that I didn't trust them or anything, I just had to make sure that I had a handle on it first myself. As I drove towards the restaurant I just began to pray. I believed that if this was the right time then the Lord would work it out. The parking lot wasn't too full. I went inside expecting to be the first one there, but to my surprise Marva and Dessa were already there. "Hey girls" I spoke as I sat down. Dessa scooted over so that I could sit next to her in the booth. As usual we started in with solving the problems of the world. We were eating, laughing and talking when Dessa asked me about what I had been doing? Are you working on another project? She asked. She knew that I always had something going on. "As a matter of fact I do. Let me tell yall about it, I said.

I wanted to ease into the conversation but for some reason I just put it out there. "I have been looking for my natural father". Silence covered the table like a clean fresh white tablecloth that had been laid down at a spaghetti dinner. All of a sudden nothing that we had been talking about was important. Marva and Dessa both looked at me as though they were searching for an expression that would give them a clue as to whether or not I was serious. Marva broke the silence with the question "Why?" I mean I know that you said that you never knew him, but why are you looking for him now. Are you sick? "No girl" I replied. "I just have this need to, if I can, to find out about him. I am curious as to what he really looked like and what he was like, or if I have some more sisters or brothers. If he liked to travel, you know stuff like that. My mom gave me some information, but I always got this feeling that it wasn't the complete story. I have some ways that are like my mother, but some things about me, I feel, came from my father. I just think that that information would bring closure to some unanswered questions that I have been wondering about for years.

"Girl, you are fine just like you are" Dessa interjected. "You not knowing your father may not have been God's intended plan, but that ain't on you. God still ordered and directed your life. You are here now because of his divine plan and purpose for your life. You are complete in Christ. What happened or happens in your life is of no surprise to Him. Who you are, what you are like is all a part of his divine design. There is nothing missing in you because your father was not there. I understand wanting information, but are you saying that you want to see if he is still alive? Getting information and actually wanting to see him are two different things". "I think I want to do both", I said. "Really" Dessa sounded surprised. "I will settle for as much information as I can get. However, if he is alive I would like to meet him face to face. A face to face would give us the opportunity to lay all of our cards on the table. I could see him, he could share his side of the story, I could ask the questions that I wanted and I could get a sense about him." "Okay", Dessa continued, "but what are you going to do with all the information once you get it? " Yeah", Marva said, "What if you find out that he is alive but doesn't want to meet you, then what? Would you be able to settle for getting information from other people concerning him and then just walk away? What if he has a lot of baggage? " "Whoa, I appreciate all of your questions and I knew that you would have many. That is why I wanted to make sure that I had a handle on it first. I actually hired a private investigator to do the search. I gave him as much information as I could. He has been at it for a while. A few months ago, he informed me that he had tracked down someone that could possibly be my father", I said with a certain amount of confidence. I got a mysterious card and picture in the mail. Then I got a phone call and now I am just waiting to see if anything becomes of it all. I am playing it safe. I know that there are a lot of weirdoes out there.

We sat and talked a little more. They listened intensely. I knew that Marva and Dessa would ask the hard questions, so I had done my homework. I just wanted to be transparent with them and solicit their support. I was not an impulsive person. I was the kind of person that investigated the investigator. This was just something that had been on my plate for a while and now I needed to eat it up or clean it off. I was not seeking their approval because I was already in the thick of it. This was major for me. I knew that this could have an impact on my life. I was praying every step of the way. I believed that knowing as much as I could about him would help me to understand more about myself. That's all. I wasn't looking for any daddy daughter relationship, no catch up on lost time, I just wanted to embrace the part of me that came from him, my father. We continued to laugh and talk. We discussed the best case scenario down to the worst. I didn't feel uncomfortable or worried about whatever the outcome would be. I knew that my girlfriends had my back and that the Lord was leading in the front.

It was getting late. The lunch hour had become the dinner hour. We had eaten and drank everything that was on the table. Now we were making the dinner mints our dessert. Realizing the time, we had prayer at our table, and then we started saying our goodbyes as we headed for the door. We always made sure that each of us got into our cars and that they would start before we pulled off into our different directions.

Chapter Twenty-one

I took a deep breath as I turned away from the sunlight shining through the window. I wasn't quite ready to get up just yet. It had been a long weekend. In fact the past few weeks and days were a little stressful. Putting the finishing touches on Lynn's party and the information about my father had me a little stressed. I really hadn't given the news about my father my complete attention.

As I lay in my bed, I begin to think and talk to the Lord. I still had some questions for myself. The most important one was whether or not I was really ready to meet the man that I thought contributed to my being. Part of me was excited about the prospect of meeting him. I would get to see what he looked like, talk to him and hear his side of the story as to why he wasn't there for me while I was growing up. I already knew some of the story, but there were still some gaps and missing pieces. I just wanted to put down periods in some places and fill in the gaps for those other parts. The other part of me still wasn't quite sure about it. To be perfectly honest, I didn't want to meet a man that had an assorted past that would make my present complicated. I wanted to be able to take him or leave him. I didn't want any drama! I needed to be strong enough to do that.

I thought myself back to sleep. When I woke up I was startled because I thought that I had overslept. Then I remembered that I didn't have to go to work or anywhere else for that matter. I had taken some days off from work. I was preparing for retirement and I had to take some of my leave or lose it. I was so glad to be able to retire. I had heard people say, you would know when it was time. Well, it was time. I had put in for some days here and there to kind of ease myself into retirement. I had a plan. Part of the plan was to sleep later and do some of the other things that I kept putting off because I had to work. I wanted to wake up on a rainy day and keep my pajamas on all day, if I wanted to, and it not be a Saturday or a holiday. I had some things in mind for my retirement. This was what I called a sample day.

Although I didn't have to really do anything, I rolled out of bed anyway. My mind was collecting ideas for what I could do, vacuuming, washing clothes or cleaning out a closet. I thought them over and disagreed. Instead I started with a bubble bath. A bubble bath during the day! Ahh, now this was retirement. I usually didn't even have time to take a bath. It was a quick shower with some shower gel and out the door.

Wow! That was relaxing. I used my Bath and Body Works lotion after I dried off. I wasn't kidding myself though; Vaseline was still my best friend. Then I slipped into my robe, and headed downstairs for a cup of hot tea. I made my tea and found a comfortable place on the sofa. I reached for the remote for the TV and started channel surfing. I didn't want to get hooked on Soap Operas, so I kept looking for something more intellectually challenging. It was interesting just to see what was on TV during the day. I settled for a movie channel. I thought to myself, I could really get use to this retirement life!

Chapter Twenty-two

When the movie went off, I felt a little guilty. I had spent about two hours just sitting on the sofa. I was going to have to get use to having so much down time. I laughed out loud at myself. I knew that wasn't going to happen. I was not a couch potato kind of girl. I needed to stay active and involved in something. I thought to myself since I had the time that I would check on a few sick people at church. I got the church directory and made a list. I wrote down five names; I didn't want to overwhelm myself. I started with Sister Marge. Her answering machine came on. I left her a message. Then I moved on to Sister Estelle. She picked up on the third ring. "Hello" she said. "Hello, Sis Estelle this is Sister Allis. How are you today?" "I'm doing right nice. Who is this?" "This is Sister Allis from the church," I repeated myself. "Oh yeah, how you doing baby?" I wasn't sure that she really knew who I was so I just went on with the conversation. I told her that I was just calling to check on her and to have prayer with her. Twenty minutes later after a lengthy conversation, I did that. Then I revisited my list, maybe five would be too many, especially, if I got two or three like Sister Estelle. I chuckled to myself. I laid the directory down on the counter and I saw Kevin's number that I had scribbled on a pad. Umm, I thought, maybe I would give him a call.

I piddled around the house for the remainder of the afternoon. I went to get the directory to make my last call on my list and also noticed the number that I had written down for my alleged father. Instinctively, my thoughts went back to my daddy situation. I needed to address this situation, but not today. Today, I was going to do what I really wanted to do. So, I focused in on Kevin's number, picked up the phone and dialed it. I waited. The anticipation was that of a child waiting to open up their gifts on Christmas Day. "Hello" the voice was smooth and peaceful. "Kevin, I said inquisitively, not sure if it was him. "This is Sandy". "Hey Sandy, it is so nice to hear your voice. I could sense his surprise. "Yours likewise" I said with a sigh of relief. "What have you been up to?" He asked. "Not much that would change the world" we chuckled. "I was just sitting here and thought that I would follow up on my promise to you. I owe you a coffee date. Remember? But I thought that maybe we could throw in a salad or hamburger on the side?" He laughed heartedly. Sounds good, he agreed. Alright, I continued, "What is a good day and time for you". "Let's shoot for Thursday of next week around seven-ish. My father is still here trying to gather some personal information and I want to be available for him should he need my help. When he discovered that my job was sending me here, he was excited. He told me that he was still looking for my older sister a while back. He doesn't really talk about her. But he always wanted me to know that I had a sister. Recently he told me that his leads had led him to this area. My father is such a character. I don't know whether to take him seriously or not. He loves to travel and may have just used my being here as an excuse to take a trip". "Your dad sounds fascinating", I added. "Yeah, this is just one of his projects" he said slowly. I was raised as an only child, so whenever we can connect, I try to do so for whatever the reason. "That's interesting; I have a similar project in the works like his of my own. I would love to chat with him, get some feedback and compare notes I said. "Oh, he would love that. Maybe I can make that happen" Kevin replied. I didn't want to sound too pushy so I switched gears, "Kevin do you know where the Little-Big Appetite Restaurant is on Chapel Road?" "Yes, that's not too far from me. "How about meeting me there on Thursday around 7 pm?" "That would be fine" Okay great, I don't want to hold you. I will put you on my calendar for next Thursday. "Great, thanks for calling" he spoke so politely. "Enjoy the rest of your evening", I said hesitantly. You too Sandy, then we both said good-bye. I liked Kevin; he was polished, but not stuffy. He was easy to talk to and be around. I was not attracted to him intimately, but he just seemed to be good people. At this point in my life I just wanted to have easy friendships. Some people can be too clingy and demanding. They want to always be in your space. I didn't want that. Kevin was a traveler, and so was I. If our friendship grew, maybe I could visit him in some of the places that his job sent him. So, with a sigh of relief, I marked my calendar for our coffee date.

The sun was going down, and so was I. It had been a good day. I thanked God for my journey. Food came to mind. I hadn't really eaten, so I went to the kitchen to fix myself something to eat. It would not be long before I would be on my way back to a relaxing position on the sofa for the evening.

Chapter Twenty-three

I took my car to the carwash. They cleaned it inside and out. I liked this place they did a really good job. My car was so dirty I was almost ashamed to take it there.

The days had really gone by quickly it was already Wednesday. I had spent my days, washing clothes, cleaning out closets, packing up unused stuff for the Goodwill, and ironing. I did some house cleaning, sending out cards, going to church for rehearsals and planning another event. I don't know how I worked full time and did all of the rest of this stuff. There still was plenty for me to do. I hadn't forgotten that I was supposed to have my coffee/dinner date with Kevin on tomorrow. I was excited about sitting and talking with him. The restaurant that we were meeting at was casual. It had a nice laid-back atmosphere. I wasn't sure about what I was going to wear, but one thing for sure, I would at least show up in a clean car.

I sat in the living room looking out the window. I watched the birds fly in and out of the trees. The sun was bright and the sky was clear. I begin to think about how good the Lord had been to me. As I sat there, I reminisced about my childhood. I was an adventurous child. I closed my eyes and in my mind's eye, I could see myself. I remembered climbing trees in the country and shooting marbles with my brother in the dirt backyard. I recalled waiting for the school bus in the cold and picking blackberries alongside the road. I loved paper dolls and coloring in my coloring books. I shared a lot of good times with my siblings. However, the one thing that I did not share was time with my father. That thought made me feel like I was on an airplane coming in for a crash landing. I opened my eyes, but the thought was still there. I took a deep breath and began to feel sad. At that moment, I thought that I had missed a really important part of my life not knowing him. Thank God, that thought didn't last for long! I couldn't really say that I missed out on much, to my knowledge just because my father wasn't actively in my life. I had a good life. I grew up in a loving home. I was well educated and developed into a productive citizen of society. It wasn't always easy. I made some mistakes along the way. While traveling life's highway I took some wrong exits and went down some dead end streets. I didn't always stop at the stop signs. I had to make some detours along the way. Yet, when I looked back, I knew that God had always protected, guided, and nudged me back to the right direction. I continued to sit on my sofa full of gratitude.

Tomorrow would be another day. I was looking forward to seeing Kevin. Maybe our time together would give me a chance to share with him about my quest to find my father. He was a good listener and I really wanted to get to know more about him also. I had nothing to lose. It's not like he really knew me, I thought to myself. However, if things went well, at least he would know what I was dealing with. I prepared myself for bed and crawled under the sheets. I reached for my book and begin reading. It wasn't long before my eyelids got heavy and I felt sleep coming on.

Chapter Twenty four

I felt good when I woke up this morning. I rolled over to look at the clock. I slept later than I thought. I had my morning devotions and then made my way to the bathroom. I looked in the mirror and told myself that my eyebrows needed arching. I didn't go through my entire mirror, mirror on the wall routine. I could see that there were some other areas of concern that the mirror may not have a kind response to. Laughing to myself, I thought I'd better come back to it after I took my shower and combed my hair. I didn't want today to get too busy. This was the day that Kevin and I had agreed to meet for our coffee-dinner date. I wanted to do a few things around the house and then run some errands.

I kept my eyes on the clock. I didn't want time to get away from me. I still hadn't decided on what I was going to wear. This was not really a date, date. I wanted to be relaxed and comfortable not sultry and sexy. I felt like it could possibly be a long evening of conversation. Jeans and a loose fitting casual top would be fine. I pulled them from the closet and got dressed. I thought that maybe I should put on some high heeled shoes. That thought soon left. Yeah, jeans would be fine

As I made my way to the restaurant, I listened to some music on the radio. I was excited about this evening. I looked forward to talking with Kevin and being in his company. I didn't even know Kevin's last name. Although this was what I would call a generic date, with no expectations, I still wanted to make a good impression. When I arrived at the restaurant, I was a bit nervous. I took some time and sat in my car to watch the happenings. It didn't seem to be busy. At least there wasn't a whole lot of people coming and going. I grabbed my purse and made my way inside. I loved this place. I had come here a few times with Mae and Dee. It was homey, small and intimidate, not a lot of noise over your head, dim to moderate lighting, vases of flowers on the table and comfortable seating. Most of all it had good food. I looked around to see if Kevin was there yet. I didn't see him. The hostess came to me with a wide grin. "Good evening, how many?" she inquired. "Can I get a booth for two please?" I asked. "Sure" she said politely "follow me". She led me to a booth on the side where I could see the door. "Thank you" I said. "My pleasure, your waiter will be with you shortly. I made myself comfortable and settled in. I looked at my watch, 6:50. I picked up the menu and started looking at what was on the menu. Kevin didn't impress me to be the kind of guy that would be late. I thought that maybe I needed to tell my waiter that I was expecting someone else when he came to take my drink order. As I lowered my menu and looked up Kevin was coming towards me. I gasped with surprise! I could feel my face give way to a broad smile. He was smiling also as he made his way to the booth.

"Hey lady, how are you doing? It's good to see you" he said all in one breath. "I am doing just fine" I replied. He peeped at his watch and said, "I'm right on time." "Yes you are, I like a timely man" we laughed. "Is this seating alright?" I asked. "Yes this is fine, only can I sit on that side? I want to be able to see the door in case my dad decides to drop in, I can see him. I hope you don't mind". "Sure that is not a problem" We exchanged places and sled back into the booth.

I think we both were excited. I gave him a few moments to settle in. He took a deep breath and stretched his hand across the table to touch mine and said "So what have you been up to?" Well, not much. I am downsizing my life" I smiled. "Now what does that mean? He asked as he leaned forward. "I'm trying to do less. I'm not talking about being lazy, but just trying to make better use of my time. Sometimes I'm busy but it seems as though I'm not reaching my goals."

He shook his head up and down and said, "I do. Life can spiral out of control if you are not careful. We can put more on our plate then we can handle at times. I try to keep it balanced and pace myself." Just then the waiter came to our table. "How are you folks doing this evening" he asked.

"Fine" we said in unison. "Great, can I start you off with some drinks?" Yes, I'll take water with ice. Kevin ordered a strawberry twist. "Have you had time to look at the menu?" Not really. "Okay I'll get your drinks and come back". Are we getting something to eat also? I asked. "You know this is supposed to just be a coffee date. I thought you said something about food when we talked. I did but we don't have to if you just want to drink and chat. "Oh no! "he said "I'm coming from work and I want to get something to eat." Looking over the menu we both started bouncing food ideas off of each other.

While he was still looking over the menu, I started the conversation by asking him a pointed question. So, what kind of work do you do exactly?" I am an IT Technician for the government. When they have a problem with their systems at large, I am the one they send for. I can do a small job, that's where I started, but most of the time I handle the big network problems. I service all of the government agencies. "Really" I said. "That's why I travel so much. This area gives me more of a home base for the government agencies, but they can send me anywhere. I'm not sure that I will stay here, but I had to put down some temporary roots somewhere. The assignment that they have me on now will take at least a year. I like it here. My biggest problem with moving around is that it keeps me from having real relationships. "So are you telling me that I am only going to get to hang out with you for a year?" I said sarcastically. "No, no, well yes in a way. I like your directness, I really don't know. All I am saying is most of my past relationships fizzled out after I moved on. I don't know if that says something about me or something about the people that I allowed to come into my life. So I am always cautious when I meet people. I put that right out front so that people can make their own decisions on how to interact with me. "Okay that's fair." 'Strangely enough though Sandy, I feel like I have known you forever. From the first time that we met at the church, I felt that we had something in common'. "Yeah, we both didn't want children running over our feet", we laughed out loud. "I like your sense of humor also. I tend to just let relationships evolve. If they take root or not I'm okay with it. I know I use that as a defense mechanism". "Don't you have anyone in your life that you can say that you really have a continuous stable relationship with?" "Yeah, a few people, my dad is number one. He has been my rock. I don't really remember my mom. My grandmother and my aunt, my dad's sister, pretty much raised me. My aunt never had any children. She and dad were the only children that my grandmother had, so I didn't grow up with any siblings or first cousins. It got to be lonely at times. My dad told me that I had an older sister but I never met her. I like to say that was in his other life". The waiter came back with our drinks and then asked "Are ready to order?" "Yes, we are". We placed our order and continued to relax. "Enough about me, I don't want to seem like a psyche patient. I told you, I am so comfortable with you my words just seem to fall out of my mouth." "What's your story?" he said after sipping his drink. "Well, I don't really have a story". "Oh come on, everybody has a story". "Okay then, my story is still unfolding". He smiled and said "I'm listening". "I don't want to bore you with all of the details of my somewhat complicated life. My story is not as condensed as yours". "Ah, come on it can't be that bad". "Alright then let me just give you some highlights. I have other siblings. I'm single and have one child. I'm an educator currently considering retirement and I never knew my natural father". "Okay, that's a beginning" Kevin said mildly. "I told you that it was complicated".

Chapter Twenty-five

The food was delicious. Two hours and a half later, we were still laughing and talking. I excused myself to go to the ladies room. I couldn't believe that I had opened up and shared so many details of my life with Kevin. After making my donation to the plumbing system and washing my hands, I walked back to the table. Kevin was on his phone and ending a conversation. "Is everything alright?" I asked. "Oh sure, that was my dad. He just wanted to know if I was still here. He was close by and may drop in. I hope that is okay with you." " No problem. He and I have something in common also" I reminded Kevin. "Yeah, that's right, you are looking for your dad and he is still looking for my sister". "How do you feel about that", I asked inquisitively. "I know how much it means to him. It is something that he has devoted a great deal of his life to. I am curious, but it does not consume me. I guess the old saying, you can't miss what you can't measure is true. I don't press him about it. It seems to give him a reason for being. Whatever becomes of it will be something that together we will work through". "That's a healthy attitude. I'm not sure that I would feel that comfortable about my situation" I replied. "Well you have to make some decisions. Based on our conversation you may be facing that situation at some point in your life" he reminded me. "I do agree with you on one point, I will face it when it comes", we smiled. "Would you excuse me?" he said as he slid out of the booth "it's my turn; I have to go to the men's room". While he was gone the waiter came back to the table to check on us. I sat listening to the music that was coming through the speakers and enjoyed the fragrance from the live flowers that were on the table. When Kevin returned, he looked up towards the door. Suddenly he was waving his hand like he was beckoning for the waiter to come to the table. In a keyed up voice he said, "There's my dad, I hope he sees me". I had my back to the door. I could tell that Kevin was excited though. He acted as though he wanted to go get him and then said, "He sees me". He turned back to me and asked, "Is this going to be okay with you Sandy? He knows this isn't a real, intimate kind of date." I assured him that it was okay. He stood at the end of the table. I held my head down while looking at my phone. When his father reached the table they embraced with his back towards me. He turned to look at me when Kevin said "Dad, do you remember Sandy from the party?" "Vaguely" he replied with an inquisitive look on his face. He reached out his hand for me to shake and I remembered that I could barely see his features at the party.

Kevin made room for him to sit next to him. "Do you want to order something to drink or eat?" "Maybe, I will just get a cup of coffee" he said. Kevin beckoned for the waiter while I tried not to stare at his father from across the table. "So, Kevin tells me that yall met at church" he stated. "Yes sir, it was truly by chance. We were both visiting". He chuckled, "Kevin will find a church no matter where he goes. I guess he gets that from his grandmother." We all laughed. "No need to call me sir. It makes me feel old." "Sorry, but I guess I got that from my mother." He laughed again. "I was taking care of some business and I told Kevin that I would be in the area. He invited me to come and formally meet you. The last time that we met, I apologize I was on a mission." "Yeah right, you just didn't want to let the lady that you were talking to, to turn her attention to someone else," Kevin teased. He responded with a drawn out high pitched "Well, I remember better now. That's right, my compliments to you. It was a very nice party." "Thank you" I smiled. The waiter came to the table so that he could place his order. I searched his face a little closer. I was certain that I had seen him somewhere before Lynn's party. Kevin and I continued with our small talk while his dad waited for his coffee. When it arrived, I watched him pour in the cream and sugar. Then I said to him, "I never did get your name". We are notorious for introducing our family by title and not by name. "I apologize" Kevin said, "You are right". "Herman" his dad said firmly, my name is Herman". I immediately went into a private mental state of shock! I placed my hand over my mouth acting like I was holding back a cough to keep the words that were lingering in my throat from falling out. My eyes would not blink and my breathing was altered. Could this be … I mean that was the name of the man that was on the picture that came in the mail. I could hear Kevin say playfully, "I was going to tell her dad". He then turned and looked at me. My complexion must have gone through all the shades of chocolates! I now was at vanilla chocolate because I could feel my blood start to drain from my face. He reached for my hand and asked "Sandy are you okay?" After a few seconds, I said "Oh yes, I am fine." I played it off, I lied. I struggled to resurface into reality. I caught my breath and stuttering I asked Kevin to order me a cup of tea while I excused myself to the ladies room. Again he asked me if I was okay. I forced a smile and assured him that I was fine.

Chapter Twenty-six

I n the ladies' room I went into one of the stalls. I didn't know whether to cry, shout, laugh or what! I was confused. Could I have come face to face with my father tonight? Was Kevin's father, my father also? I had so many thoughts swirling around in my head at this moment. What should I do? I had to reason with myself and get a plan. I knew that I couldn't hide out in the ladies' room for the rest of the night. How could I handle this? I wanted to confront him, but maybe this wasn't a good time. What if I was wrong? This was too much of a coincidence. How would it affect Kevin? Oh Lord, please help me with this, I cried out! I physically broke out in a sweat, my hands were shaking and my stomach was in a knot. Someone entered the ladies' room so I pushed the door of the stall open, went out to wash my face, and composed myself. I looked myself in the mirror and convinced myself that I could handle this. I took some deep breaths, opened the door and headed back to the table. When I reached the table, Kevin stood up and asked "Is everything alright?" "Oh yeah" I said. "It wasn't something you ate was it?" his dad asked. "They told me that the food was supposed to be pretty good here ". "No, I'm fine." I insisted. I wanted to get the attention off of me. I looked across the table and said "So, Mr. Herman, Kevin told me that you were visiting from out of town. What brings you to town may I ask?" "Well, I'm actually looking for someone. Kevin's oldest sister. I've been looking for her for a while and I got a lead from one of my FBI allies, a young lady that I use to work with, that she may be living in this area somewhere". My stomach was still unsettled. "Would you know her if you saw her?" "Naw, unfortunately I haven't seen her in over thirty years. It was a difficult separation, but I never forgot her". I examined his every feature. He fit the description of the man that my mother had told me about, a dark chocolate complexion man, and medium height with a firmly built body frame, medium light brown eyes, full lips and a small well shaped nose. He had a full beard and mustache which was neatly cut and trimmed. Now, as he sat across the table from me he looked like the man on that picture at age seventy. Wow, I was taking it all in. Kevin interrupted and said "You and Sandy have something in common dad". Smiling he said, "Oh yeah. What?" "You both are looking for someone. She is looking for her natural father." "Really" he said "what do you know about him". Bells and whistles were going off in my head. This was my opening, I thought. If I tell him what my mother had told me, then he would connect the dots and know that my story, was his story. Should I dare?

"Dad might be able to help you with your search. He knows some people in some high places" Kevin laughed quietly. "Now, I wouldn't say all of that, but I have made some friends along the way". Kevin pushed, "We're in no rush; share some of your information with him if you would like". I didn't want to blurt out that I think you are my father, although that is what my mouth was forming to say. I took a deep breath and said, "No, I don't want to bore you with my sad story. It has been a good evening and I don't want to spoil it." "Oh no" he said, "Your story is your story. One thing that I am good at doing is listening". I was struggling so hard to bring forth the right words. It was like walking on cracked ice, but I didn't want to miss this opportunity. All kinds of emotions were running through my inner being. I was excited, curious and a little fearful. I wanted to open the door, yet I didn't want to drag Kevin through it. Then I found myself allowing words to creep out. "Well, my mom told me that my Dad was a military man and traveled quite a bit. He wanted to see the world. He wasn't ready to settle down in one place and she couldn't take off with him. She had other responsibilities. She told him that she was pregnant before he left on an assignment. He came back a few times to see us, but not to stay." Herman raised his cup to take a sip of his coffee and looked at me over the rim of the cup. I continued. "The only concrete things that she told me about him were that he lived in Washington D.C and that he served in the Army. She didn't have any pictures of him, but she gave me a vivid description of him. I always thought that I would recognize him if I ever saw him. I've been searching for him for years on and off. I am sure that his appearance has changed down through the years," I said looking at Herman with piercing eyes. He raised his cup again and Kevin said "not much to go on, what was your mother's name? " My mother's name was, Marilyn.

Herman suddenly acted as though he was choking and needed to clear his throat. Time stood still as our eyes locked. Kevin asked him "Are you okay dad?" "Yeah son, a little coffee went the wrong way". "You never met your dad so you never got his side of the story uh?" Herman asked. "No, we moved from that area and life went on. However, I always wanted to meet him. I wondered if he ever looked for me, like you are looking for your daughter. I'm curious to know if he wonders how I turned out. I wish that he had fought harder to stay in my life. It is not always about money or material things. It is the love and the validation of that child that makes that relationship so very important. I always felt like I had some pieces missing. Although, I had a good life and the Lord has blessed me every step of the way. I don't feel whole in a natural sense."

"Interesting," he said as he rested his cup in the saucer. "Our stories are similar and I wonder if my daughter is bearing some of those same emotions. See my daughter doesn't have the whole story either. She doesn't know that I loved her from day one. Even before I saw her my heart loved her. Although her mother and I couldn't have a regular relationship, I wanted to be in her life. I wanted to see her grow. I wanted to hold her hands, and kiss her cheeks and hear her laugh. I wanted to spoil her and make her feel special. When I got back from my last tour, she and her mom had moved. I tried to get information on their whereabouts, but to no avail. It broke my heart, like I am sure it probably broke your dad's heart not to have you in his life. But like you said after a time, life went on. However, because I love her so deeply I can identify with what you said about missing pieces, I still search for her." "Wow dad, I never knew how deeply you felt about this, Kevin whispered. "It wasn't your burden to bear. I loved her in my heart like I loved you openly for the past thirty- some years." Tears were now welling up in his eyes as he casted a glance in my direction.

Kevin reached for the napkin on the table to give to him. I could see that he was feeling the emotion that his dad was experiencing at the moment.

"Oh my goodness!" Kevin exclaimed looking at his watch, Sandy it is late and I need to get you home by a decent hour" forcing a grin to his lips while firmly rubbing his dad on his shoulder. Suddenly I felt bad about sharing my story. I didn't really want to hurt him, but I did want to take the chance to subtly drop some clues if in fact he was my dad. Yes, I guess you are right. It has been a great evening. I looked at Herman one more time to examine his facial features and to mentally compare them to the photo that I had at home. We all slid out of the booth. The restaurant was nearly empty. We made our way to the cashier and the waiting area in front of the restaurant. "Give me a moment; I will take care of the bill" Kevin said. "I can pay for myself" I said. "I wouldn't hear of it, maybe next time" we agreed. As I stood outside in the waiting area, I wanted to continue the conversation, but I thought that if Herman was my dad he would have connected the dots by now. Maybe he had and just didn't want to say anything right now. When Kevin opened the outer door he asked me where I parked. I chuckled and said, "That question sounds familiar". He said "yeah right! Okay Dad if you want, you can wait right here for me. There are some benches over there. I am going to walk Sandy to her car and bring my car around to pick you up". "Okay son", he nodded.

Kevin was checking his pockets for his keys before he went through the main door. I turned and took a few steps back. Extending my hand I said "Thank you Mr. Herman for sharing your story with me. I feel like we do have something in common". I let go of his firm grip and softly said, "By the way my last name is Allis". He lifted his head straight up from looking down at the floor. He looked directly at me and in the same breath before he could give a reply I said, "Oh there was one more thing that I forgot to mention. Kevin was still preoccupied with trying to find his keys. My mom said that my father had a small tattoo of a bulldog on the inside of his left arm." Suddenly he grabbed his chest with both of his hands and stumbled back to sit on the bench. Kevin turned and left the door to rush back to him. "Dad, are you okay, what's wrong? Speak to me dad, what's wrong, should I call 911?" he questioned him with concern. Herman was shaking his head no, while using one of his hands to reach for me. I came close. Kevin said "I think I need to call for an ambulance. "No", his dad said sternly with tears running down his face by now. "You are her! You are Ca-san, Sandy my daughter!" he spoke softly but deliberately while looking right at me. He grabbed my hand and pulled me close. "It can't be, I don't believe it. Thank you Lord! I thought that I would never find you," he cried out. He was pressing my head to his shoulder. I was crying now too. Kevin was still asking questions. "What? What do you mean dad? Sandy what is going on? I don't understand". For a few seconds, Herman and I just embraced. That waiting area had become our own private sanctuary. Years concerning our search probably flashed in our minds collectively. When I pulled away, his dad asked him to sit down. He tried to composed himself and said through his tears and trembling voice "this is your sister". Kevin was bewildered. "What are you talking about, what do you mean, what are you doing?" He was wrestling to pull his arm from out of his shirt. "Kevin" I injected "my story is your dad's story. We have been looking for each other and finally the facts have come together tonight. What a coincidence or should I say that this is our God-wink moment. This is the Lord's doing. "Are you alright Mr. Herman?" He smiled, "Why so formal". "I mean do you need some water or something" I asked. "Water no, maybe something a little stronger" he replied. "Dad I don't understand", Kevin was still seeking information. "I know you don't son. This is a miracle" he said after catching his breath. He sat straight up on the bench. "Let me try to explain. Sandy was before you, she was connected to a life that I couldn't live at the time. Before I left on my last tour of duty, I got this tattoo. Look here. I showed it to her mom and I assured her that even though the odds were against us, I would keep fighting for us to be together. You know Bulldogs can be stubborn. She had to tell Sandy about the tattoo. How else would she have known about it? The short version is this; this is the daughter that I have been looking for. This is your sister". Kevin looked at me still in disbelief. "Are you telling me that all of this time I was in the presence of the sister that I could hardly get you to speak about?" "Yes", he said with tears rolling down his cheeks again. I reached out to grab Kevin's hand. "Maybe that's why we connected from the very beginning. We are kindred spirits" I added. Wow! Kevin was speechless. "After all of this time, here you sit before me. You were never a secret, but he never went out of his way to make you the main topic of conversation. I knew that you were a missing part of his life. I am overjoyed for him, and glad for you. I don't know what I am for me yet" he said shaking his head. I said, "I know it's a lot to take in, but for right now just know that the details speak for themselves and they are true. Let's all just breathe".

We were still sitting in the foyer, but internally I was having a one-way conversation with myself. I discovered early in my life that I was different. I never really fell into a deep depression or went through any emotional or psychological changes around not knowing who my real dad was. I wasn't bitter or angry. I didn't go through the stages of acting out as they say. Of course you had to know my mom to know that she wasn't going to stand for that! When I got to the age where having a dad would make a real impact on my life, my stepdad was with me. He filled a lot of the voids in my life. I believe that was God working in my life even then. My mom made sure that I had a balanced life. I didn't waddle in self-pity. I gave it some thought at times and then I would just stop thinking about it. Knowing who my dad was wasn't a need but more of a curiosity. I knew I was created by two people. Therefore, I knew that I had some characteristics that came from each of them. Some people really go through some changes about this very issue. Not having my dad in my life did not define who I would be. I just thank the Lord that his hands were on me every day. The Lord made it so that this issue would not be an issue for me. This is not a sham or get over scheme. It is not fake or an accumulation of false facts. It is real. It is unbelievable, but it is real and too much of a reality to be a coincidence." Herman broke the silence when he said, "This is nothing short of a miracle! We will not absorb all of this tonight. Let's just take a few days to let it all seep in and then we can get back together again. " "That sounds like a plan" Kevin and I agreed.

I stood up, poised myself and looked them both in their faces. With a deep breath I said, "If we are to believe the facts, you are my father and you are my brother. I am the one that you have known about and have been searching for. Growing up, I could identify with the little girl that the Supremes sang about in their song Love Child. My mother was a nurturer; my step-dad became a provider. You need to know that God made me a strong, independent woman. With him, I have weathered many storms. I've been in valleys and on mountain tops. I've had victories and suffered defeats. My search for you has been intensive. Most of the time, I was disappointed with the results. We are at this moment now because

God, my heavenly father, has ordained it to be so. Yes, you were not there in the flesh. I, like every child, wanted their natural mother and father in their life. As I grew into womanhood, and I looked back over my life, I realized that I always did have a mother and father. I was always covered and cared for by God, the Father". I managed to exhale and specifically turned towards Kevin and said, "Kevin, I know you have just as many questions as I do. But for now just know that I believe that the Lord has answered our prayers."

The lights in the restaurant had dimmed. The staff was cleaning up and preparing for the next day. The restaurant was closing. Oddly enough I felt at peace. I could finally put a period in this area of my life. Tomorrow would be the beginning of a new chapter in each of our lives. What seemed to have happened so quickly tonight was in reality a lifetime of happenings. Finally, I could put a face on me. I could now come to grips with my emotions, thoughts, fears, behaviors and attitudes. The why was no longer a mystery. Together Herman and Kevin stood up quietly. Through tear stained faces, we all three hugged in a huddle for a moment. We said our goodbyes softly, and went through the main door of the restaurant. Kevin asked his dad, *our dad*, to wait for him in front of the restaurant. I walked in the direction of my car. I could not resist turning around to take another glance at the man that I believed to be my father. Kevin walked me to my car in silence, but instinctively we both knew that … *I was my father's daughter.*

NOW

I am a completed work, as I stand before you today
I remember my struggles; I didn't start out this way
Experiences have taught me how to live and survive each day
I'm stronger, bolder, smarter and more at peace, I must say

I've cried in the morning and sometimes late at night
I felt like I was losing ground, but I had to stay in the fight
I had to keep the faith and keep the prize in sight
While accepting who I was, whether wrong or right

The Lord has always kept me, no matter what I was going through
He is my heavenly father; he controlled my earthly fathers too
All my needs were supplied, my wants were very few
He gave me strength to excel and have a positive view

I'm not depending on someone else to validate who I am
My steps have been ordered by God, my light cannot be dimmed
Each day I am reminded, of in whom I've put my trust
So this life that seemed deficient is now a life full and robust

I'm thankful for my journey, for those that were present and absent too
The gifts, the skills and talents, all the information that was new
It helped me become my own person and strengthened me as I grew
My outlook is better now and life has taken on a different view

About the Author

*S*andra Allison- Belford is an unmistakably blessed child of God. She is the youngest of five children, a mother, grandmother, and a proud great-grandmother. By profession, she is a retired educator for her local public school district and a licensed cosmetologist. In 2005, she added the title of published author to her list of accomplishments with her book of poetry, entitled "Say It Out Loud". She is the recipient of many honors and awards including, Outstanding Teacher of the Year, Phi Theta Kappa Outstanding Academic Achievement Award, and a nominee for Who's Who Among American Teachers. She is an active member of the Huber Memorial Church located in Baltimore, Maryland. She is enlightened by her past, engaged in her present, and excited about her future. She claims no glory for herself, but acknowledges Jesus as her Lord and Savior and gives Him all the glory and honor for making these things and more, possible in her life.

Printed in the United States
By Bookmasters